PSYCHO SHOP

ALFRED BESTER

Alfred Bester was born in New York in 1913. After attending the University of Pennsylvania, he sold several stories to *Thrilling Wonder Stories* in the early 1940s. He then embarked on a career as a scripter for comics, radio, and television, where he worked on such classic characters as Superman, Batman, Nick Carter, Charlie Chan, Tom Corbett, and the Shadow. In the 1950s, he returned to prose, publishing several short stories and two brilliant, seminal works, *The Demolished Man* (which was the first winner of the Hugo Award for Best Novel) and *The Stars My Destination*. In the late 1950s, he wrote travel articles for *Holiday* magazine, and eventually became their Senior Literary Editor, keeping the position until the magazine folded in the 1970s. In 1974, he once again came back to writing science fiction with the novels *The Computer Connection*, *Golem^{100}*, and *The Deceivers*, and numerous short stories. A collection of his short stories, *Virtual Unrealities*, was published in 1997. After being a New Yorker all his life, he died in Pennsylvania in 1987, but not before he was honored by the Science Fiction & Fantasy Writers of America with a Grandmaster Award.

ROGER ZELAZNY

Roger Zelazny authored many science fiction and fantasy classics, and won three Nebula Awards and six Hugo Awards over the course of his long and distinguished career. While he is best known for his ten-volume Amber series of novels (beginning with 1970's *Nine Princes in Amber*), Zelazny also wrote many other novels, short stories, and novellas, including the award-winning *Lord of Light* and the stories "24 Views of Mount Fuji, by Hokusai," "Permafrost," and "Home Is the Hangman." Zelazny died in Santa Fe, New Mexico, in June 1995.

PSYCHO
SHOP

PSYCHO
SHOP

ALFRED BESTER
& ROGER ZELAZNY

INTRODUCTION BY GREG BEAR ⋅ A BYRON PREISS BOOK

VINTAGE BOOKS A DIVISION OF RANDOM HOUSE, INC. / NEW YORK

A VINTAGE ORIGINAL, FIRST EDITION
July 1998

A Byron Preiss Visual Publications, Inc. book

Edited by Janna E. Silverstein

Special thanks to Keith R.A. DeCandido, Kirby McCauley, Martin Asher,
J. Edward Kastenmeier, and Emily Epstein

Library of Congress Cataloguing-in-Publication Data
Bester, Alfred.
    Psychoshop / Alfred Bester and Roger Zelazny : introduction by
    Greg Bear —1st ed.
        p.   cm.
    "A Byron Preiss book."
    "A Vintage original"—T.p. verso.
    ISBN 0-679-76782-7
    I. Zelazny, Roger.   II. Title.
    PS3552.E796P78   1988
    813'.54—dc21   98-6111
                        CIP

Book design by Iris Weinstein

www.randomhouse.com

Printed in the United States of America
10   9   8   7   6   5   4   3   2   1

PSYCHOSHOP: SF JAZZ, B TO Z

By Greg Bear

Without Alfred Bester and Roger Zelazny, we would not today have William Gibson or Neal Stephenson, perhaps not even Terry Pratchett or Douglas Adams.

Bester and Zelazny were among the SF jazz greats of their time. Each whirled in like golden dust-devils and disrupted the science fiction landscape, blowing new tunes in new styles and tempos, leaving glitter-speckled, disheveled admirers and a great many imitators in their wake. Other writers puzzled out some of their riffs, and improvised a few new ones of their own; but the surprise and originality of B and Z could not be duplicated.

Alfred Bester began writing in the forties, but it was in the fifties that he made his mark, just as science fiction novels were being published with fair regularity in hardcover, and at the beginning of the golden age of the SF paperback. His SF appeared sporadically through the sixties and seventies: then he seemed to fade. At the time he was declared a Grandmaster by the Science Fiction Writers of America, he was practically broke, dying, almost forgotten by the mainstream SF reader. Even with the highlights, his was not a career to be fervently desired—but it was very like the career of many musical jazz masters.

To list all the jazz masters of SF is difficult, and I'm certain to leave out many worthies. Stanley G. Weinbaum belongs, I think; Fritz Leiber, Henry Kuttner and C. L. Moore, Theodore Sturgeon, Frederik Pohl and C. M. Kornbluth, Edgar Pangborn, Robert Sheckley. Ray Bradbury has been accused of being pure Sousa, but I think he's a jazz master as well.

Roger Zelazny, along with Samuel R. Delany and the quizzical Philip K. Dick, dominated the jazz style of the sixties, then settled in through the next two and a half decades to a solid, productive career with frequent, often short, award-winning masterworks. His career was long (though not long enough), disciplined, remunerative, and full of improvisations, collaborations, surprises: a career to be admired. He did not live long enough to be declared a

Grandmaster, but no matter; that's a sometimes haphazard glory.

After Bester's death, Zelazny was offered an interesting opportunity. Bester had left behind an unfinished SF novel; would Zelazny finish it? He took up the challenge, and the result is unique—*Psychoshop*, a posthumous duet between two masters of SF jazz, a rollicking, sometimes cold, sometimes hot torrent of riffs that splatters in style and flavor across the decades.

Like cool modern jazz, the tone is skewed, even perverse. The characters are breezy and practically affect-free, the epitome of pulp heroes, fifties style; they sometimes tell us what they feel, but we don't ourselves feel it. The mood is wry, fast, exhilarating, but ultimately downbeat. The book is meant to make you grin, but with a shake of your head; laughter with an edge. Bester laid down this tempo, but it was not at all difficult for Zelazny to pick it up and draw it out. Zelazny, after all, was one of Bester's literary children; what Bester pioneered, Zelazny made his own country. The match is almost (though not always) seamless.

Looking over a copy of the original manuscript is fascinating, and it's too bad it can't be reproduced in facsimile, with commentary. The typewriters change here and there, there are many handwritten corrections (but in whose hand? Bester's, perhaps; Zelazny's mostly, or an editor's?) and there are the trademark Bester sketches and typographic flourishes. Students of both writers should secure a bootleg copy (not from me!) and analyze the process in more detail.

Writers like Bester and Zelazny enrich a field and provide the intellectual nutrients for intense growth, for all kinds of writers. My own style might more aptly be described as classical, with dips into avant-garde, but I love the jazz greats of SF. Their writing is a tart sorbet between heavy courses. It dissolves greasy, maudlin pretense and cleanses the palate.

Psychoshop: a dark acid curio, brisk, fast, memorable, a rare improvisational duet from two of our best.

PSYCHO
SHOP

ONE · THE PSYCHBROKER

I was looking around desperately when my boss, Jerry Egan, poked his head into my office and in his soft Virginia voice asked, "May I come in, Alf?"

"Sure. Sure." I went on searching.

He hoisted himself on a corner of my big table (I hate desks) and watched. Then, "What have you lost?"

"I can't find my goddamn passport."

"Tried pockets, raincoat, travel bag?"

"Three goddamn times."

He started sorting through the mess on my table, stopped abruptly, and loafed to the low bookshelves under the window. He picked up my British motoring cap and there it was.

"How in the name of heaven could you go right to it?"

"My father was a dowser."

"Bless your father! Bless you!"

"I'd like to spring another foreign assignment on you, Alf. In Rome, but it's tricky. Ask around about the Black Place of the Soul-Changer."

"Sounds wild. What is it?"

"No one really knows. Girl of mine was there but she wouldn't talk about it. Sort of ashamed."

"Any suggestions?"

"You know how to dig. If it's just saloon-hype to pull the jet set trade, forget it. If it's a place that's doing the impossible, like inventing new sins, give it the full."

"Any leads from that ginzo girl of yours?"

"She did drop one name, Adam Maser. That's all."

"Isn't a maser some kind of microwave gadget?"

"You tell me, Alf. You're the Yankee genius. I'm only the Dixie chaser."

The world is divided into 99% civilians and 1% elite. The civilians are all running scared, afraid of nonconforming. The elites are on easy terms with themselves and the world, don't give a damn for, and can't be spooked by, anything. So when word got around that I was in Rome doing features for the chic *Rigadoon* magazine, I was accepted by the jet set and aimed in the right direction.

So there I was on a stool alongside this Adam Maser in La Corruttela having drinks and bar-chatting. I'd been told that he was the mysterious Soul-Changer and naturally anticipated meeting a Frankenstein or Count Dracula or even the Phantom of the Opera wearing a mask. I couldn't have been more wrong.

He was tawny red, almost the color of a leopard, the hair darker red than his skin, which simply looked sun-and-windburned. His slitty eyes were jet black. His fingernails were pointed and ivory-colored, but his teeth were brilliant white. Altogether an overpowering figure.

When we first sat down with each other, he had taken his time sizing me up, then introduced himself, and I did likewise. He said he'd heard about me. I said I'd heard about him.

His manner was all charm and grace; pure café society. He laughed a lot and his chuckle was almost a purr. He had an easy voice but was slightly hesitant in speech as though continually searching for the right word. Wonderfully pleasant and wide open like all the other one-percenters who don't give a damn. I figured him for a delightful interview provided his Black Place made it worthwhile.

"Adam Maser's an odd name," I said.

He nodded. "It's a compromise name."

"Between what and what?"

"We're late twentieth century, right?"

"And that's an odd question."

"I've got to be careful, speechwise. You know all about passing through time zones when you travel; jet lag and all that?"

"Uh-huh."

"Well, I also travel through people and culture zones, so

I've got to be sure I'm talking the right language. Can't speak Aztec to a Druid. Tell you about it some time if you're interested."

"Tell me about the compromise."

"Well, the name should really be Magfaser."

"You're putting me on."

"No, Magfaser's an acronym."

"Of what?"

"Maser Generated Fetal Amplification by Stimulated Emission of Radiation."

"Jeez."

"Yeah. Only close friends call me that.

"And Adam because I'm the first turkey— Do we say turkey in the late twentieth?"

"Not anymore."

"The first to be amplified during the embryo caper. Caper's right, isn't it? I'm having a little trouble getting with late twentieth. Just come from a session with Leeuwenhoek and a long seventeenth-century Dutch discussion about microscopes."

"You need warming up." I called the bartender. "Double shot for me, please, and anything my good buddy Maser Generated Fetal Amplification by Stimulated Emission of Radiation wants to order."

That broke him up. "You're a right rigadoon, Alf."

"You're fairly OK yourself, Adam. What were these friends unknown amplifying you to do?"

"Damned if I know. I don't think the lab mavens know either. They're still trying to find out, which is why they've got me under observation, like in a terrarium. . . ."

I shook my head. He was sounding flakier by the minute.

"They thought they were doing a linear magnification, sort of putting me through a magnifying glass."

"Sizewise?"

"Brainwise, but what they did was multiply me by myself into a quadratic."

"Inside your mother?"

"Hell no! I was a test tube clone floating in a maser womb."

"So where is this terrarium where the good doctors have you under observation?"

He purred a chuckle. "My place. If you want to come, I'll show you."

"Love to. The Luogo Nero? The Black Place?"

"That's what the locals call it. It's really Buoco Nero, the Black Hole."

"Like the Black Hole of Calcutta?"

"No. Black Hole as in astronomy. Corpse of a dead star, but also channel between this universe and its next-door neighbor."

"Here? In Rome?"

"Sure. They drift around in space until they run out of gas and come to a stop. This number happened to park here."

"How long ago?"

"No one knows," he said. "It was there six centuries before Christ, when the Etruscans took over a small town called Roma and began turning it into the capital of the world. If you were looking for the Luogo Nero, where the sinister Soul-Changer did business, you were told it was just opposite Queen Tanaquila's palace. Usually your informant would then spit three times to ward off evil."

I smiled. "When did you get put into it, the black hole?" I asked.

"About a thousand years from now, your time. For me, ten rotas back."

There has to be a limit. "Adam," I said, "one of us is crazy."

"And you think it's me." He laughed. "That's why I'm safe when I tell it like it is. No one ever believes me."

"I've been assigned to do a story on you."

"Sure. I guessed. I'll cooperate; give you the full; but *Rigadoon* will never print it. They'll never believe you. You'll be wasting your time, Alf, but you'll have some wild stories to tell. So come on, already."

Outside, the redhead flagged a cab and told the driver, "Il Foro etrusco." As we got in he said, "That's what they call the ruin of Tanaquila's palace, the Etruscan forum. I'm just opposite. If I gave a driver my address he'd swear he never heard of it and tell us to get lost."

The Etruscan forum looked like any ordinary Roman ruin, a few acres of fenced rubble covered with the usual graffiti:

DeeDee and Joe's
Smithfield Eatery
U.S.A.

Rip 'em Tear 'em
Skin 'em alive
Pennsylvania '35

Across the Via Regina from Tanaquila's, the Black Place looked like any ordinary Roman house except that it stood alone, flanked by empty, weedy lots. Evidently no one cared to live alongside. It was built of the flat Roman brick three stories high, with windows and balconies, some with wash hanging from them.

"Windows, balconies, wash, all fake to conform," Adam said. "Also the bricks. They aren't the clay types; they're baked bort, cheap diamond dust, to last forever. Come into my web."

We stepped into the entranceway.

The sign above the door wasn't the traditional hockshop logo, the three gold balls, allegedly the arms of the Medici family but actually invented by the Lombard pawnbrokers as an attention-getter. No, what the sign sported was a fantastic extrapolation: three gold horizontal 8s, symbols of infinity. A nice touch. Its motto was Res Ullus—Anything.

"Petrified ebony," Adam said, rapping the door with his knuckles. "Also to last forever." He swung the door aside.

"No locks?"

"Open day and night to all the world. My observers want me to react to everybody and everything. Might help them figure out what my quadratic is. And that's why they made the terrarium a hockshop. It's a universal crossroads."

"You must have been ripped plenty."

"Never. The goniffs think this is a Mafia H.Q. and are afraid to mess around. Too bad. Lately, your time, the terror clowns've been tossing bombs which can't do anything against diamond and ebony. God knows who they think I am."

There was a pleasant foyer with a wide rack for hats, coats, and such, and an enormous brass scuttle containing a colorful assortment of walking sticks, umbrellas, parasols, all probably forgotten by visitors. He led me into a giant reception/living room which would have made collectors, curators, and dealers green with envy. Exquisite rare furniture, lamps, books, prints, and paintings; cut crystal and objets d'art; an inlaid harpsichord; an Aubusson rug, 20 × 30; linenfold paneling; a magnificent ironwork stairway leading to the upper floors; inexplicable items which had not yet been designed and built in my time. And . . . AND, standing in the center was a woman. . . .

Gleaming black hair, sharp features, and tiny ears were what I noticed first. Her eyes were golden, oval, and never blinked, so wide apart she could almost see behind her. The tip of her tongue constantly darted just inside her narrow lips. Her skin was quadroon but seemed to glow with iridescent mica flakes when she moved forward to greet us.

"This is Alf, my new buddy," Maser told her. "Alf, this is my nanny."

"Nanny!?"

He nodded. "I'm just a kid."

"But— I— This is too much for me. Does your nanny have a name?"

"I call her Medusa."

"Medusa?"

"Uh-huh."

"You have to be kidding!"

"Of course." The redhead chuckle-purred. "It's our joke because she's descended from our snake genus. I don't have to explain why she calls me Macavity, the Mystery Cat."

"No need. Good evening, Ms. Medusa." I gave the enchantress my best bow. "Do you have a real name I might call you?"

"Ssss."

I looked at Maser.

"That's her real name," he said.

"Good evening, Ms. Ssss."

He broke up and she flashed a smile at me.

"What have I done now?"

"You called her Glory Hallelujah."

"No."

"Yes. Ssss. Ssss. Can't you hear the difference?"

"Not really. It's one hell of a language."

"We come from one hell of a universe. You should hear the pisces crowd bubble. Talk twentieth Yank to him, Nan." She flashed another smile but that was all. "No, no, Nan. Alf can't hear UHF. Try lower."

Her voice came, smooth and tingly like the low notes of an oboe. "Good evening. So nice to meet you. . . ." She took my hand. Hers was cool and firm. "I'd like very much if you called me Glory, Alf."

"Hallelujah," I muttered.

"Careful, you're turning into stone," Macavity laughed. He crossed to one of the panels, which proved to be a door. As he started to open it he said, "It's quite dark, Alf. You won't be able to take notes."

"Never do. I've got temporary total recall. Lasts about an hour. When I leave you I'll go back to the hotel and get it on tape before it fades."

"I see. Tell you what, I'll swap your temporary for permanent. No charge. On the house."

"You can do that?"

"Sure, if you want to. No sweat. I've got a beauty from an idiot savant. You know the type: I.Q. nowhere but a memory down to the finest minutiae. He traded in his recall."

"For intelligence?"

"No. You won't believe this. Instruments for a one-man band, come in for the Grand Tour. Hold the fort, Nan."

Most of us have seen a hockshop at one time or other, from the outside and even inside. I did a full feature on pawn-shops for *Rigadoon* once. Their slogan is: If it isn't alive and you can get it through the door, you can hock it. The only word for them is clutter. They display everything from A-alembics to Z-zithers, but this Black Hole pawn-cum-psychshop . . . !

It was an endless black cavern piled with physical As to Zs and covered in a blizzard of New Year's Eve confetti and streamers. They weren't bits of colored paper, they were psychic moietiés that had been pawned or sold.

They were particles of living souls charged with energies that try to make themselves known to us through our clumsy conscious senses: sight, sound, smell, taste, touch, kinetics. This timeless Libido Exchange was a kaleidoscope of Man's rejections and desires, discontents and remedies.

Sexual images predominated: penis, vulva, buttocks, breasts—large, small, pointed, blunt—and scores of erogenous zones. Sexual acts: hetero, homo, bestial, nymphomania, satyriasis, and all the erotic postures of desire, passion, lust, love, and pleasure.

Strength and beauty: muscle, stature, form, grace, skin, hair, eyes, lips, color. Power: over men, over women, over events, over selves. Success: in love, life, career, leisure. Brilliance: intellectual, political, artistic, social. Status. Celebrity. Popularity. Perpetuity.

And a chaos of fears, fixations, hatreds, beliefs, superstitions, salvations, manias, plus fragments from the far future and dim past which had no meaning for me. All this I saw, felt, tasted, and touched. I was flayed by this shrapnel from the battle between Man's realities and yearnings. I was shattered.

Adam's voice came. "Spooky, isn't it?"

I could make him out through the dark turmoil; his crimson was curiously luminescent. All I could do was croak.

"You all right, Alf?"

I didn't respond. I couldn't. Something farther down the way had caught my attention, held it. Without thought or will I continued to move in that direction.

"This isn't real space, as you know it," said Adam. "We're protected by several layers of tricks. But even so, you are headed in the direction of the singularity. Go too far and it becomes dangerous. Go farther, and there's no turning back."

"Uh-huh," I said, and I kept going.

"You're still well within the safety margin, of course, or I'd have stopped you. In fact, you're only nearing the stripping field where I remove those traits or talents customers wish to dispose of. The adding field is off to the left—there's a kind of symmetry involved in the way I engineered it. That's where I install those things they're trading up to—or down to. We've got to bear a little to the left now to pass safely between them. Just follow the illuminated claw marks. Wouldn't want to be stripped indiscriminately. Not by a field, anyway."

I plodded on.

"The fields also grow stronger the farther you go," he continued. "I don't really work with them much beyond this point—"

I halted. I froze. I made some sort of noise in my throat.

They hung there, as I had detected them subliminally from much farther back: human forms, bodies suspended as if from meat hooks, swaying, turning, limp and lifeless, as in some steady breeze. There were seven of them.

"What," I croaked, "are they?"

"Seven guys," he said, "who traded everything they had."

"How? Why?"

"In each case, the man gained access here while I was out of the room. He wandered into the stripping field—you saw how easy it was to do—and it took away everything he'd added to himself since birth. What you see are the remains, breathing—albeit slowly—and with very faint heartbeats. The field's time-effects preserve them. As Shelley said, 'Nothing beside remains.'"

"When did it happen?"

"The first one, Lars, lived back when the Etruscans were in charge around here. Marcus came a few centuries later. Erik was a Germanic mercenary. And we've a Vandal and a Goth and a thirteenth-century Norman Crusader," he said, gesturing. "The last guy, Pietro, was sixteenth century. Claimed to be a painter."

"Why do you think they did it?"

He shrugged.

"Maybe simple curiosity. I can understand curiosity. More likely, they wanted more than they thought they could afford and figured they might find a way to rip me off. You want that memory job now?"

The nearest body was turning in that eerie breeze. Its profile began to come into view.

I screamed. I turned. I began to run.

"Alf! What's the matter?"

His hand fell upon my shoulder, steering me safely between the fields. His question rang in my head. But already I was blotting out—the horror.

"What is it, man?"

"It— It startled me. It was like— I don't know."

"Uh-huh. It's quite an experience the first time around. You'll get used to it."

"I'm not sure. I'm so damned empathic."

"That's the price the artist has to pay."

"And this is the real Black Hole?"

"Oh, you've been in it since the front door. The foyer and reception are decorated to put people at ease. This is the undisguised real thing."

"It's more of a Hellhole."

There was a dazzle of light as the door to reception opened and closed. Glory's voice came. "Client, Dammy."

"Great, Nan. Alf can watch us in action. Where from and when?"

"A college boy from the U.S. Early nineteenth century."

"What's his problem?"

"Something about asthma."

"I'm no M.D., but let's see what we can do."

The client was seated but stood up politely when we entered the reception room: a skinny college boy in his late teens, dark, pale skin, big head, melancholy eyes, dressed in the post-Federal style.

"How do, sir," Maser said pleasantly. "Nice of you to wish here. We're all on a first name basis. This is Nan, my assistant; Alf, my associate. I'm Adam. You?"

"They call me Gaffy in college," the boy said. His speech

was unusual and quite charming; Southern spoken with a slight English accent.

"And you want to pawn or buy what?"

"I want to exchange my asthmatic wheeze for something endurable."

"Ah, you have rales, eh? What makes them unendurable, Gaffy? Are they too loud, too prolonged, painful, what?"

"They speak to me in a language I can't understand."

Adam's jet eyes widened. "Now that's a new one on me. Are you sure it's a language?"

"No, but it does sound like words in sentences."

"Most interesting, Gaffy. Permit me to listen." Without waiting for approval, Adam bent and put an ear to the boy's chest. "Deep breath, please, and let it out slowly."

Gaffy obliged. Maser listened intently, then straightened, smiling. "You're quite right, my dear boy. It *is* a language, early-eleventh-century Persian." He turned to me. "There's no end to fantastic phenomena, Alf. Our client is wheezing passages from the *Shah Namah*, the epic fantasy by the great poet, Firdausi. It was the source for Scheherazade and the *Arabian Nights*."

I stared. Gaffy stared.

"Now I'm not a physician, so I can't remove the wheeze," Adam continued briskly, "and I refuse to exchange it. It's a treasure you'll appreciate and thank me for some day. What I will do is sell you a knowledge of Persian so you can understand what you're hearing. Self-entertainment, as it were. Inside, please."

We were seeing Macavity at his most Napoleonic. Arguments and objections were out of the question. It was something he'd referred to as his persona power. As the college boy followed Adam into the Hellhole, I looked at Glory.

"If Maser's just a kid, what'll he be like when he grows up?"

"God, maybe?" she answered. "He doesn't overwhelm me but to tell the truth, Alf, he's been whelming me lately."

"D'you think that this persona power is his quadratic?"

Before she could reply, Maser and the college kid came out.

"What?" I exclaimed. "So quickly?"

"Moments, real time," Adam smiled. "No counting, psychwise. There's no time or dimensions in the libido and intellect."

"Xirad zän Pahlavi." Gaffy beamed.

"No, no!" The redhead was overpowering again. "It was our agreement that no one is to know you understand ancient Persian. Questions will be asked and how can you answer them? You damn well better keep your word."

The boy nodded submissively.

"Right. Got any money on you?"

"All paper, sir. A dollar Federal and two-fifty Bank of Richmond."

"I'll take the paper half dollar for my fee. I'm not undercharging you. It'll be worth a hell of a lot more in the future."

"Thank you, sir."

"Now pay attention. When you go through the front door think hard of the place you wished yourself here from, and you'll wish back into it. Same time. Same place. Got it?"

"Yes, sir." The half-dollar bill was handed over. As the boy turned to leave, Glory said, "Do you want a receipt, Mr. Gaffy?"

"No thanks." He hesitated, then, "Gaffy's what they call me in college. I hate it. My real name's Edgar. Edgar Poe," and he was gone.

Three jaws dropped. Then we burst out laughing.

"So that's what inspired him," I said.

"And you think *Rigadoon*'s going to print this?" Adam chuckled.

"I have my doubts. I also have doubts about Poe's work. Wasn't it a cheat, really?"

"No way, Alf. You ought to know. Inspiration's one thing; what you do with it is something else. Firdausi's been translated into a dozen other lanauages. Same source for all. Has anyone else ever equaled Poe?"

"God knows they've tried. Me too. But never."

"I had another thought about him," Glory said. "Perhaps this is why he took to drink and drugs. It must have been hell, living with that stockpile and trying to re-create what he could remember."

"Ah yes, memory," Adam said. "Come back into limbo, Alf, and I'll replace your temp recall with that permanent from the one-man band. Like I said, on the house. No charge."

"I pays my own way." I was all class. "I got fifty liras burning a hole in my pocket."

"A whole nickel U.S.? Like wow! You're the last of the big spenders."

"Naw. I'm on expense account."

But just as we reached the door to the Hellhole, Glory called, "Another client, Dammy."

"Oh? Where and when?"

"From the Beta-Prometheus Cluster. Twenty-fifth."

"Jeez," I said. "Does it have two heads?"

"Shut up, Alf. What business, Nan?"

"His name's Tigab. He wants to get rid of an obsession. Says he imagines he's haunted by a hitching post that's in love with his wife."

Glory was ushering the client in as we returned to the parlor. I whispered to Adam, "If I went through the door now would I be in that Cluster in the twenty-fifth?"

"You'd be where and when you really wanted to be," he murmured. "Not just dreaming. We'll fill in details later." Aloud, to the client, "Good evening, sir. So nice of you to wish here from so far off. You've met Nan, my assistant. This is Alf, my associate. I'm Adam, the psychbroker."

Not two heads, just one, and a marked resemblance to the classic portraits and busts of Shakespeare. Two arms, two legs, wearing a timeless jump suit.

Adam continued, "Now what's this delightful obsession about a loving hitching post, Mr. Tigab?"

"Well, it's like this. Me and the wife made our pile and thought we'd live it up a little. We bought a mansion from the estate of an antique dealer, furnished and elegant like this room."

"Thank you, Mr. Tigab."

"Elegant outside too. You know, gardens, lawns, trees, driveways, and 'longside the front steps is an antique hitching post."

"Forgive me, Mr. Tigab, but why do you talk like that?"

"Talk like what?"

"Three words level and one word down."

"Oh. We're born that way out in the Cluster. You know, like kids are born righties or lefties? We're also born inflecting."

"I see. All with the same inflection?"

"Oh no. All different."

"Anyway," Mr. Tigab continued, "about this hitching post hangup I want wiped. We got settled in and everything was great until one afternoon we're sitting in the parlor when my wife jumps up and yells, 'There's a man looking through the window.'

"I jump up. 'Where? Where?'

"She pointed. 'There.'

"I look. Nothing. 'You imagined it,' I told the wife. She swore she saw him and he was some kind of ghost because she could see trees through him.

"Well, she's got imagination—she always wanted to be a poet—so I paid no mind, but she kept on seeing it all the time and damn if she didn't start me thinking I was seeing it too."

"Yes? How did you see it?"

"We were sitting by the fire in my study, talking, when I saw this dumpy little spook come in and sit down alongside my wife. It was the image of the figure on the hitching post."

"And?"

"I kept imagining I saw it coming in and sitting with my wife, looking at me like it wanted to be me. She's got me believing this damn delusion and you've got to kick it for me."

"You're sure it's the guy from the hitching post?"

"The image."

"What's it look like?"

"Real antique. Hundreds of years. Hell, I'll draw it for you. Got some white paper?"

Glory produced a large pad and pencil.

"No," Tigab said, "we don't use pen or pencil in the Cluster, we project. Just hold the pad up where you can see it."

He pointed a finger and the hitching post took form on the pad: an eighteenth-century figure, dumpy, right arm raised, left behind its back, top hat on the back of the head, high collar and loose ascot, long overcoat, unmistakable scowling face.

Adam and I looked at each other and began to sputter.

"What's so funny?" Tigab demanded.

"The hitching post ghost," Adam said. "It isn't a delusion, Mr. Tigab, it's a genuine spirit, and it isn't in love with your wife, it's facinated by how you speak to her."

"I don't believe it. A ghost likes what I say to my wife?"

"No, it likes how you say it. Your inflection. If you'll come with me I'll solve your problem by selling you a new inflection. No more spook sitting with your wife listening to you."

More or less dazed, Tigab followed Macavity into the Hellhole while Glory and I grinned to each other, shaking our heads.

A vaguely familiar-looking man in mirrorshades, sweat pants, and a red and white polo shirt walked in. I watched him in the mirror. He was about my height and build, his reddish hair was close-cropped, and he had on some sort of moccasins or dancer's shoes. He wore studded leather straps about his wrists.

He approached Glory. "Is the proprietor in?" he asked.

"Yes, but he's occupied," she replied. "May I help you?"

"No, thanks," he said. "I'll catch him another time."

He turned and left, soundlessly.

When they came out of the Hellhole, moments later,

Tigab was so stunned that he could barely mumble. All the same, his new inflection was equally unmistakable. My grin broadened.

"Got to pay up and go home. The wife's got to get used to my new singsong. Me too."

He pulled a pouch from a pocket, opened it, and dumped green pebbles on a table. "Cluster coin-of-the-realm," he grunted. "Take as many as you like. You earned it and I'm obliged."

They were raw, uncut emeralds. Adam picked up the smallest stone and returned the rest. "This is too much, Mr. Tigab, but since you say you've made your pile I won't feel too guilty. Nan?"

I followed Glory as she escorted Tigab out. He was humming. When we returned, we three looked at the hitching post portrait.

"I've seen blackamoor posts," I said, "and jockeys, but what demented designer used Beethoven for a model?"

"Like I said, Alf, there's no end to fascinating phenomena in this world. D'you think *Rigadoon*'s going to print this?"

I shrugged it off. "And I spotted what you replaced those first four notes from Beethoven's Fifth Symphony with."

"Did you?"

"Yes I did now; the main theme from 'Rhapsody in Blue.' Is Tigab going to be haunted by the ghost of George Gershwin now?"

"All depends on the hitching posts," Adam laughed.

"If I understand it correctly, there's got to be an exchange. Why can't you just remove some unwanted aspect of the psyche?"

"The danger," he explained, "is squatters moving in on your psychique, Seele, nao-tzu. Farstayst? Had a woman once with a wild idea; she wanted to leave a vacanza, a vacancy, in her heart for her lovers. I went along with it to see how it would work out.

"But a damn black widow spider nipped in ahead of her studs and that was that. Oh, sure, every living thing, animal or vegetable, has a soul. Never again. Borgia, her name was. Lucy Borgia."

The front door was suddenly enveloped by a pillar of cold, corposant fire. It advanced into the reception room and out of it stepped the towering figure of Mephistopheles.

We had to give him a big hand.

He bowed graciously. *Merci! Merci! Merci!* I am the tenth Count Alesandro di Cagliostro."

"Ah yes," Adam smiled. "Descended from the original Cagliostro, adventurer, magician, liar, cheat. Died in the fortress prison of San Leo in 1795."

"I have that honor, M'sieur Maser."

"The tenth Count Alesandro? Then you must be from the late twenty-first or thereabouts, eh?"

"Paris. Early twenty-second, M'sieur."

"Welcome. We're honored. This is—"

"Your assistant of the serpents, Ssss." Apparently he pronounced it properly. "But this gentleman from les Etats-Unis I do not know."

"Alf, from *Rigadoon* magazine. He's associating with me while he prepares a feature on the Black Hole Hockshop."

"Delighted, M'sieur Alfred. I felicitate myself. You know, of course, that your admirable writings will never be received as fact. Who could believe the magique wrought by

M'sieur Maser, eh? Yet he is as genuine as my great-great-etcetera grandpapa was— Pardon, Maître. How does one translate *simulateur*?"

"Faker."

"As the grandpapa was a faker."

"Thank you, Count Alesandro. I hope this is a social call, we'll amuse each other. Dr. Franz Gall, who developed phrenology, paid a social call. Said he wanted to explore the bumps on the head of a charlatan. I was amused but he wasn't."

"Why not?" I asked.

"He was dumbfounded. Said I had no bumps at all, which threatened to undermine his entire theory. I started to reassure him with a— How does one translate *craque*, Count Alesandro?"

"Tall story."

"With a tall story about my brain being where the bowels usually are, and vice versa. Said I was a freak and offered to let him feel the bumps on my belly. He left in a huff."

We laughed. Then Cagliostro said, "So sorry to disappoint you, Maître, but I am come on an affair of business. I wish to purchase these," and he handed Adam a cassette.

Adam pulled the end of the tape out and began running it between thumb and forefinger. The tape seemed to be composed of flickering fireflies. Cagliostro caught my curious stare and said, "Phonotact of the twenty-second. There are in all six hundred and sixty-six items."

Adam whistled softly. "The Number of the Beast in *Revelations*, six hundred, threescore and six. Are you going to brew a beast, Count Alesandro? A warlock's familiar, perhaps?"

"You forget what follows: *Let him that hath understanding count the number of the beast: for it is the number of a man.*"

"Quite right. Then you're making a man."

"An inconnu, unheard-of man."

"Curiouser and curiouser."

"I intend to synthesize an android unique. Not the clumsy simulacrum that laboratories cook, but a brilliance which can communicate with and control the deepest wellspring of human behavior, the primal layer of motivation. No, not an android, my friend."

"An Iddroid!" Adam said, eyes seeming to flash. "But this is fabulous! Your grandpapa, nine times removed, may have been a faker, but you are a genius absolute!"

"A thousand thanks, Maître. Then you will help me?"

"I insist on helping. I'm grateful for this splendid challenge. Have you any idea of your chances for success?"

"*Chacun la moitié.* Fifty-fifty."

"Good enough odds for me. Now, about what you require for your Iddroid synthesis; I have many of the items in stock, but I shall have to go out and locate others. Just to mention a few: a sixth sense, scrying by aggression, a freak superstition, an inconnu absolu, and—this number's a killer—origins of Humanity's Collective Unconscious."

"All essential, Maître, and I'm prepared to pay handsomely."

"No way, Count Alesandro! I'm collaborating for the glorious defi. Now, *est-ce que cela presse?* Are you in a rush?"

"No hurry at all."

"Can you give me a week?"

"I shall give you two or even longer. Au revoir," and Cagliostro exited in a pillar of purple smoke.

Before I could express my astonishment the red Macavity's persona power took over. "Ready, Nan?"

She nodded. He was certainly whelming her.

"Right. We'll be in and out, Alf, jumping to and from times and places. You mind the store."

"Hey! Wait a minute! I can't monkey around with psyches. I don't know how."

"Of course not." To Glory, "Don't forget the tape." To me again, "Just stall the clientele till we get back."

"Stall them? How? I'm no linguist. What if a dejected Druid comes in?"

"Fake it, Alf," he laughed. "Fake it with chutzpah. Go the whole nine yards."

And they were gone.

And before I could decide whether to keep the kettle boiling or get the hell out of there, the hitching post né Ludwig van Beethoven (1770–1827) came tramping in storming German.

Jeez.

"Me no speakie kein Deutsch," I faked. "You, du, efsher, dig der Ingle-itch?"

He felled me with a scowl, strode to the harpsichord and banged three octaves, probably to help him shift gears, and then growled, "Dot verdammt Shakespeare. His schatten, ghost haunted mich und give mir schöne, beautiful inzpiration. Dies ist dein fifth. G-G-G-E flat. Dis ist your fünste. F-F-F-D. All in key of C Minor. Wunderschön!"

"Would that be fifth as in symphony?"

"Ja! Ja! Fünste symphonie. I listen to ghost waiting for more, wanting to komponieren, compose, und suddenly cursed schatten change inzpiration."

"How?"

"Kein more Fifth Symphonie in C Minor. Now verdammt Shakespeare ghost zing me halbton, flat tones, flat-
ted dritte und fünste und siebente, thirds, fifths, sevenths.
Blue intervall. Mit synkopieren! Unheard of! Ausländisch!
Verrückt! Ein Symphonie in Blau!"

Oy gevald.

TWO · THE $HOPING LI$T

He was gnawing on the outside bort bricks," I said, "and when I asked him what he wanted in fluent Swahili, he dropped dead."

"Probably couldn't stand your accent," Adam grinned, inspecting the bod. "He looks like nothing. Complete John Doe. Any ID on him?"

"I didn't search. Just hauled the corpus in out of sight and waited for your glorious epiphany."

"Check him, Nan. A brick-chewer ought to be interesting." Ms. Ssss silently began a rather gloomy inspection. "Now give me the full, Alf. What were you doing outside? Taking a runout powder? Dereliction of duty?"

"No way. I don't deny that I was considering it but the hitching post came charging in."

"What? Not the late, great Ludwig B.?"

"Beethoven in the flesh-ch, storming about his ghost making him compose a Symphony in Blue."

Adam guffawed. "Oy gevald!"

"My very words."

"How did you handle it?"

"I psyched him."

"Go on!"

"I scout's honor did."

"Not in there," pointing to the Hellhole.

"Right out here, at the harpsichord, and I wonder what your observers are making of it."

"*Cela m'importe peu*. Tell all."

"It was easy. I hummed, sang, one-fingered on the keyboard all I could remember from his fifth. He began to shake with excitement, said I was his new inspiration, and jotted it down on slips of score paper. I escorted him out, him blessing me in Deutsch, and there was the brick-chewer."

"Alf, you're the genius absolute. Did the late, great offer to pay?"

"Too inspired, but I collected anyway."

"How?"

"I pinched one of his notes." I handed Adam a slip of score paper on which were scribbled various measures with *Allegro con brio* and *Andante con moto* and the initials *LvB*.

"Jesus, Mary, and Joseph!" he exclaimed. "This is worth a fortune! I'm thinking of taking you on as a permanent partner, Alf."

"Never mind that. Why isn't Glory talking to me or looking at me? Is she angry? Did I do something wrong?"

"No, no, she's getting ready to molt and that always depresses her."

"Molt? Shed her skin?"

"Right on. She's from the serpent crowd, remember? She never knows what her new look will be and she worries."

"But snakes don't change, they just become more than they were before."

"So does Nan, but she worries all the same."

"I don't see how she could possibly be less magnetic."

"Uh-huh. She's got you in her power."

"What about you cat people? Do you have problems, too?"

"My God, yes! A raunchy song goes with it." And Adam sang:

> *Cats on the rooftops, cats on the tiles.*
> *Cats with syphilis, cats with piles.*
> *Cats with their assholes wreathed in smiles,*
> *As they glory in the joys of fornication.*

"With Glory?" I admit I was jealous.

"With my nursemaid? My guardian? Are you mad? Never! Anyway, I'm only attracted to cat-type girls."

I felt better. "So where, when, and how long were you? It's only been a couple of hours, here-time."

"New York. Twenty-fifty. A week."

"So it's still standing."

"More or less."

"Get anything for the Count's Iddroid?"

"Yes, by God! A sixth sense. It's like precognition."

"If it exists. I know women claim they've got intuition."

"Oh, it's real, Alf. I've got some beauties in stock. One's from Doc Holliday, which is why he got kilt in the OK Corral."

"The gunfighter? Why'd he dump it?"

"Said he knew he was going to die soon anyway. Just didn't want to know the exact time and place. But I'm talking about an omnichronosense that enables you to see up and down the Arrow of Time, past, present, and future, simultaneouswise."

"Impossible!"

"Which is why Cagliostro will dig it."

"Where'd you find it?"

"To quote you, in the flesh-ch."

"Quoting right back at you, tell me all."

"About five years ago," Adam obliged, "this guy came in with a portrait of himself painted by a fashionable artist named Van Ryn. He was from the States in the early twenty hundreds, and he was scared out of his wig because Van Ryn had depicted him as 'Le Pendu' from the Tarot fortune-telling cards: The Hanged Man, slung upside down from a beam with a cord around one foot and his hands tied behind his back. Dead.

"The client wanted me to probe him and find out if he had some hidden savage criminal streak which would earn him this frightful punishment. If so, he wanted it wiped. It was crazy, but I explored him and found nothing more dangerous than a yearning for adventure. So I sent him back to twenty-thirty and thought no more about it.

"Until a few years later, when I learned from one of his contemporaries that the client had died in an awful accident. He'd taken up skydiving—that adventure yen—and when his chute opened he'd gotten tangled in the cords, upside down, and smashed to the ground head foremost. How could this Van Ryn have called it in advance, even though he painted the scene differently?

"So when I spotted a sixth sense on Alesandro's list I thought maybe this Van Ryn had something like that and was worth a try. Went off to the Big Apple up then and covered museums, galleries, art schools, and found out the following.

"Victor Van Ryn was, is, will be a magnificent and successful artist. He was born Sam Katz, but that's no name for a fashionable painter. Victor suffered from cognitive astigmatism."

"What's—"

"Wait for it, Alf. Wait for it. Physical astigmatism is a distortion of the eye lenses that causes rays of light from an external point to converge unequally and form warped images. This is what afflicted El Greco and caused him to paint elongated faces and figures.

"But the challenge for the portrait painter is to see through the persona mask of the subject into the true personality, and put them both on canvas, the outward and the inner. This insight requires a sensitive, perceptive cognition. Van Ryn had it but it was astigmatic. He saw the past, present, and future of whoever or whatever he was painting and got mixed up.

"He didn't know what to believe so he settled for painting everything he perceived, past or present or future and sometimes all together. Clients got sore as hell at being depicted as decrepit ancients or embalmed corpses in a coffin. He even painted one as a small boy engaged in what the Chinese call 'hand lewdness.' Naturally, they refused to pay.

"The end came when Van Ryn received a secret commission from a presidential candidate to paint the secret pleasance of his secret mistress, and Van Ryn produced a bijou of her in the garden of same, naked and en flagrante with another lover. You don't dast mess around with powerful politicians and their popsies.

"We tracked him down at last. What made it tough was that he'd gone back to his original name and original Bronx, which was a ghetto. He was camping on the top floor of a low-income housing ruin, scraping a living by lettering sales signs for stores and posters for protesters. A damn bad scene."

Glory broke in quietly. "I've finished, Dammy."

"Great. Any ID on the brick chewer?"

"Nothing, except two negatives."

"Such as?"

"No chance of using fingerprints. He has no loops, whorls, anything on his fingertips."

"But that's impossible," I argued. "Even the apes have primitive prints."

"Not our friend here." But she didn't answer me; she only spoke to Adam. "He's a complete blank. Take a close look."

We looked. She was right. I've never seen a more anonymous blank. There was no outstanding feature. He was beige and doughy, the way an android might look before the final processing.

"The clothes, too," Glory continued. "All new, cheap, misfits, unidentifiable."

"Stolen maybe?" Adam suggested. "Or a charity handout? What's the second negative?"

"He had nothing in his pockets except a shopping list."

"But that could be a hot lead, Glory," I said.

"No way." She was still speaking only to Adam. "Not when you've seen this list," and she handed it over. Printed on a scrap of what I could have sworn was parchment was:

$HOPING	PLEA$E
¢	.35
$i	.25
Mn	.25
W	11.00
¢r	3.00
Fe	85.15

Underneath was a drawing of a hexagonal cruller and a Ping-Pong ball.

"I'll be damned," Adam wondered. "Mysteriouser and mysteriouser. Didn't you tell me you were the Yankee science type, Alf?"

"Uh-huh. Straight A's at Brown."

"Ah? Rah-rah Brunonia. I suspected you were an Ivy League gent. So what is your scientific deduction, my dear Holmes?"

"Whoever put this list together was kind of weak on spelling and the letters C and S."

"But what do the letters stand for?"

"They're chemical symbols, Watson. Carbon, silicon, manganese, tungsten, chromium, iron. The numbers with them are percentages."

"All adding up to . . . ?"

"The proportions of tungsten steel, the hardest tool steel known."

"My word, Holmes! Merely to make crullers and Ping-Pong balls?"

"Not quite, my dear Watson. He was shopping for tool steel nuts and ball bearings. What's more, he probably couldn't speak any of our languages, hence the graphic list to speak for him, and didn't know that he'd have to pay, no money of any sort on him. He's an alien from nowhere that we know."

"Brilliant, my dear Holmes!"

"Add him gnawing the bricks outside, Adam, and you've got a mystery on your hands that only Sam Katz can solve."

"Indubitably. Good old past, present, and future."

"When you bring him in we'll have him draw a picture of this bod and that'll tell all."

"Except for one hitch."

"What?"

"He won't come."

"Why not?"

"Didn't like my offer."

"Which was?"

"The vision of any famous artist in exchange."

"Oy. Wrong offer, Adam."

"How so?"

"Look, I've been dealing with artists and photographers

all my professional life and I know that the one thing they want most is to make what we call a new sound—in their case, a new vision. They never want to do what's been done before."

"Proceed, Alf. Proceed cautiously."

"Go back and grab him with a new sight."

"Such as?"

"A wider vision of things as they are."

"But Picasso's done that, and Chagall, and Jackson Pollock, and—"

"That's just subjective. I'm talking about a wider physical vision, up into the ultraviolet, down into the infrared, even further if you've got it in stock from anything from anywhere."

"And I do. I do. Macavity the Mystery Cat's got everything. Alf, your boss was right. You're the science absolute. You've got to join us. In the meantime, mind the store. Let's go, Nan."

"I can't." Her voice was weak and she looked strangely pale.

He gave her a warm smile and said gently, "I see the change is on the way. Not to worry. Wait for us. We'll be back in a flash. Come on, Alf. I'll need you to help haul Van Ryn. If you're game just wish along with Mac the Cat."

"Right with you, old buddy," and I sang, *"Alf on the rooftops, Alf on the tiles . . ."*

As Adam led me up the desolation that had been the Bronx's Grand Concourse, a man passed us on the street, staring, first at Adam, then—much longer—at me. He had on mirrorshades, mocs, sweatpants, a green and white polo shirt. Also studded leather wrist straps. His hair was red and nowhere over an inch in length. I remembered him from the shop, back when Adam was in the Hellhole with Mr. Tigab. At first the man looked as if he were going to speak, but after studying me again—neat beard and mustache, engaging smile, and all—he seemed to change his mind. He swung on by. I was about to point him out when Adam said, "Here we are."

Adam's brief description of the falling-down housing project had left out the horrors. The apartment complex stank of excrement and rot, and as we climbed to the top floor I saw dead bodies sprawled about, dead dogs roasting over open fires, naked kids who might as well have been dead. And the noise! The tumult!

The Katz–Van Ryn apartment was a relief. It had a locked door with a peephole and when at last it was opened for us the place looked clean and neat and smelled fairly fresh. The walls had been painted with bright abstracts and the broken flooring had been converted into what looked like charming labyrinth puzzles.

"You again." The artist growled.

"With a new sales pitch." Adam unleashed his leopard magnetism. "May I introduce Alf, my partner? Alf, this is Maître Van Ryn."

We gave each other the once-over-light. I was wondering what he saw in me with his past, present, and future sixth sense. I know I was laughing at myself for what I saw. Because of his real name I'd anticipated a Borscht Belt character. He was closer to General de Gaulle, moustached, tall, and strong. Fortyish.

"Which would you like to be called?" I asked, friendly-like. "Sam or Van?"

"What the hell do you care?"

"Just getting acquainted. I've been an interviewer and feature writer most of my professional life, and I've found that a way of reaching people is through the name they prefer. I was doing a feature on a most distinguished Knight of the British Empire. Dame Judith. She was rather careful and standoffish until I asked her the same question. She did a take, laughed, and told me that when she was a kid her nickname was Frankie. We got along fine after that."

He laughed too. "When I was a hotshot they used to call me Rinso."

"Rinso it is."

"What's yours?"

"When I was a college jock they used to call me Blackie."

"Blackie it is." That seemed to ease him. "Now what's the new sales pitch he's talking about?"

Another gimmick in interviewing is to find a mutual enemy. In this case it had to be poor Adam. "Pay no attention," I said. "He can't understand creative professionals and never will, which is why I reamed him out and came to see you. I know you're blocked and what you're going through. I've been there myself."

"Blocked hell!" he growled. "I'm finished."

"Uh-huh, we always think so, which is why artists have to stick together and why I want to back you. You've got too much talent to waste, and we both know that everybody thinks they have talent—'I could write a great story if I only had the time'—but very few actually do."

He nodded. "They've all got delusions, Blackie."

"My very first girl, Veronica Renahen, a freckled redhead, used to cry herself to sleep nights because she was a genius only nobody would admit it. She was all of twelve."

He laughed, took my arm, and seated me alongside him on a bench, ignoring Adam, who quietly took a stool in the corner. "Did you bang her, Blackie?"

"Hell no. I wanted to but didn't know how."

He laughed again. "Same thing with me. I wanted to be a merciless mercenary but didn't know how."

There was a sidetable with neat, clean glasses and decanters. He poured two drinks, still ignoring the villainous Adam, and we drank together. It was a very nice peach cordial.

"Old Man Renahen ran a deli in our neighborhood," I chatted. "His favorite story was about a Jewish lady who came in and asked for liverwurst. He took a big one out of the cooler, stuck the open end in the slicer, and began cutting. After a dozen slices he asked 'Enough?' She said, 'Slice more.' After another dozen he asked, 'Enough?' She said, 'More. More.' When he was halfway through he said, 'Enough now?' She said, 'Now I'll take ten cents' worth.'"

Katz–Van Ryn roared with laughter. "But of course! Of course! She wanted to make sure it was fresh. Typical! Typical!"

"And there's a fascinating parallel with us," I went on. "We only see ten cents' worth of the total spectrum, smack in the middle. As one artist to another, wouldn't it be sensational if we could see all the way from one end of the liverwurst to the other—the whole nine yards?"

"My God, Blackie! What an idea."

"Which is what I'm offering you."

"What!"

"In exchange for your sixth sense."

"Are you serious?"

"Dead earnest, Rinso, and we can do it. Think, man!

What could your talent do with a vision that extends beyond the ultraviolet and infrared? No more past, present, and future hangups. No more rages and feuds. You can get back to your real work and create what's never been seen before."

"My God! My God!" He was staring into space. "To paint the aura of people and things, their vibes, radiations, unconscious receptions and perceptions, ESPs . . . Picasso tried but he was just guessing . . ."

"And you won't have to guess."

"You're not putting me on, Blackie?"

"Look at me, Rinso. Read hard and deep. I'm wide open. Look into me and decide."

We made intense eye contact for at least a minute, never blinking, until his eyes rolled up to heaven and his big body seemed to sag. "You're telling it true," he whispered at last, "though there's a lot of fog blocking parts of your life. I think you've saved me. I don't know how I can ever pay you. It's a deal. What do we do now?"

"The Black Hole," I said. "Rotten Adam Maser will lead the way."

As we came in through the ebony doorway I was so intent on the Who What When Where Why of the brick-eater which Rinso Van Ryn might discover that the scene in the reception room came as a shock and nearly stripped my gears.

The corpse was propped upright in a gold brocade wingchair sort of like a mythical king on a throne, and at its feet lay a Nubian slave girl. Only she wasn't Nubian, slave, girl, or alive—she was the empty, sagging skin of Glory Ssss. The lower body was whole but the upper was in tatters. Evidently the renewed Glory had wriggled out that way.

Macavity took it in his stride, went to the foot of the iron stairway, and shouted up, "Nan, we're back."

From above came the sound of a shower over her reply. "Be right down, Dammy." Her voice sounded a little higher in pitch, more clarinet than oboe, and I wondered what the rest of her newdom would be like.

"Don't be too long. Alf, the pitchman absolute, has brought back our artist."

Rinso tore his eyes away from an amazed inspection of the room and demanded, "What the hell is going on in this museum?"

"Tell him, Blackie."

"The deal stands just as agreed," I said. "No ifs, ands, or buts. Your sixth sense in exchange for ultra-vision. Fair enough?"

He nodded.

"We'd like to ask a favor before Macavity removes your sixth sense."

"What favor?"

"Use it one last time."

"Use it? On who?"

"That body."

"Holy Moses, you're all crazy in here," he growled. "I'm getting the hell out."

"Wait, Rinso. Let me explain." And I told him about the brick schtick and the mystery shopping list. Not boasting, I'm a pro and know how to sell a story, and Van Ryn was grabbed. He gave me an approving punch on my shoulder.

"You're the one, Blackie," and he crossed to the kingly corpse. Adam and I waited while he concentrated on it for long minutes. At last he turned, shaking his head. "Nothing, Blackie, but nothing."

"Because he's dead?"

"Because he's completely unreal. Out of this world. Same like him," and he pointed to Adam. "Yeah, I cased him, too. Another weirdo from nowhere. You sure keep crazy company."

More crazy company swept down the stairs to join us, the new Glory, even more staggering than when I'd first met her. She was lighter, more octoroon than quadroon, and the mica flashes of her skin had become odd glows when she moved, as though reflecting rosy spotlights. There were streaks of silver in her hair, and the great golden eyes were hypnotic.

And I was hypnotized. Adam saw it, chuckle-purred, and made genteel introductions as though we were all meeting for the first time. After a warm greeting to the equally stunned artist, Glory turned to me.

"My kid sister told me all about you, Alf." She gestured at her shed skin.

"Glory Hallelujah," I responded.

"She's your boa, Blackie," Rinso burst out.

"What?"

"I saw her in your future when I cased you."

"His feathered boa to decorate him?" Glory laughed. "I'd like nothing better."

"No, lady, his boa constrictor." To me, "I saw you two tangling and strangling together."

"*As they glory in the joys of fornication*," Adam hummed. "Enough already, Maître. Come into my den of iniquity and I'll consecrate our contract." He shot me a perplexed brow-lift. "Do we say 'consecrate' in the late twentieth, Alf?"

"I think you're reaching for *consummate*."

We heard no warning from the outer door but the dead man's identical twin oozed in. He was wearing a raggedy sweatsuit and had a black box hanging from his neck. He took a quick pan, then pressed a button on the box.

"Parlatta Italiano?" it squawked. "Sponishing? Ingleeze? Frenesing? Dansk? Germanisch?"

"Etruscan," I said.

"Shut up, Alf. English would be best for us, sir. Greetings and welcome."

Another button. "I sank you. I see my brudder get here too lately."

"May I ask where you're both from, and why?"

A lightning survey of Adam from head to toe. "Haha. Hoho. Another parallelogram like usly. Which cosmos you?"

"Far futurewise."

"We past. We call The Hive. What you?"

"We call ours The Zoo. How'd you come through?"

"Hole same like here."

"Where?"

"Numero quatro planet."

"So there's another hole on Mars to another neighbor. More wonders. What is your name, please?"

"Name? Name?" A complete blank.

"Termites!" Rinso exclaimed. "That's what they are and that's why I can't scan anything from them. They're only parts of a colony."

"I see. Thanks, maître. Tell me, sir, why did your hive brother come looking for steel objects?"

"Needly to digest."

"My God!" I broke in. "Gizzard stones! Of course. And that's why he was trying to chew off the bricks. Diamond bort is even harder than tool steel."

"Enlighten me, Alf."

"We have life forms that swallow hard stones to help the gizzard fragment food to make it digestible. We've found little heaps in the fossil remains of dinosaurs, dodos, and giant emus. Some species are still doing it today."

"Correctly. Correctly," the box agreed. "No stones the brudder. Starving deathly. None left in hive so come for help."

"Too late, I'm afraid," Adam said. "What now, sir?"

"Must take back."

"Ah? You bury your dead in your cosmos?"

"No bury. Eat." And exit the termite carrying his lunch, leaving an appalled silence behind.

"No wonder they need gizzard stones," I said.

"D'you think he might have tried to eat us?"

"Not without your diamond dust."

"Please, Blackie," Rinso pleaded. "I've got to get out of this freakshow. This is no place for a nice Jewish boy from the Bronx."

"Right, Rinso. Go with Svengali and let him do his thing, but I'm warning you: once you've seen his psych-shop, the artist in you won't want to leave."

Adam ushered Van Ryn through the paneled door into the Hellhole, closing it behind them. Glory picked up her shed skin, folded it carefully, and bore it away upstairs. Shortly thereafter, I heard the sound of hammering. Then she returned and sat down on the couch alongside me and took my hand. Hers was still cool. Mine was trembling. She didn't say anything. I couldn't.

At last, "Part of your charm, Alf, is that you don't come on macho with women."

"I'm the chicken-type with girls."

"But not with men. Dammy told me you were spectacularly charming with that artist."

"He told you? I didn't hear him."

"UHF."

"Oh."

"And now you're doing it to me."

"No, Glory, I'm not even trying. God knows I want to, but I know I'm not in your class."

"And that's how you do it. You let us make the first move. That's your stranglehold."

I was going to ask which of us was boa constricting the other when the psychbroker and the artist came out of the Hellhole, Katz–Van Ryn pleading, "Just a little more time, please. Just a little longer. The visions in there are—"

"Enough to kick you back into your real career." Macavity's persona power was in full charge. "When you're back at work you can come any time to recharge, but then you'll have to pay."

"Anything! Anything!" Almost gushy with gratitude. Then the artist stared at us with his magnified vision. "Holy Moley! There's an aural glow around you two that— And a mingling neural borealis and—"

"And don't talk your new sight sense," Adam commanded. "Paint it. Come on, Nan. Let's schlep this nova back to New York to dazzle the art world. Mind the store, Blackie—" He gave me a puzzled look. "How the devil did you get that nickname? You're a brownie, not meaning a Girl Scout."

"The last name. Noir. French for black."

"But of course. Do they pronounce it French style back home?"

"No, they sort of rhyme it with foyer."

"C'est domage. Right. Ready for the liftoff, Rinso? Avanti artista!"

Glory brushed my palm with her lips and thank heaven

the nova didn't see what that did to me. As they started out the front door Adam called, "We may be a little longer. I think there's something else up there that Cagliostro needs for his Iddroid. By the way, there's a magnifying glass in the top drawer of the Welsh dresser."

"What? Why?"

"Someone's left a minigift on the front step. See what you can make of it. Here it comes."

The three disappeared as a tiny champagne bottle came rolling into the reception room. It was an exact miniature, the cork and label, about the size of a medicine bottle. On the bottle were the miniature letters: OLD BOND LTD—but as I examined it with the naked eye I saw that it contained no wine. Through the dark green glass I could make out a tiny roll of paper.

THREE · S.O.S. IN A MINIBOTTLE

I got the magnifying glass from the Welsh dresser, finally managed to fish the tiny roll of paper out of the miniature champagne bottle, and read:

18 Dec. 1943: Still camping alongside the Round Pond in Kensington Gardens. I'm afraid we're the

last. The scouts we sent out to contact possible survivors in St. James's Park, Earls Court, and Brompton have not yet returned. Dexter Blackiston III just came back with bad news. His partner, Jimmy Montgomery-Esher, took a long chance and went into a Hammersmith junkyard hoping to find a few salvageable amenities. A Hoover vacuum cleaner got him.

20 Dec. 1943: An electric golf cart reconnoitered the Round Pond. We scattered and took cover. It tore down our tents. We're rather worried. We had a campfire burning, obvious evidence of life. Will it report the news to 455?

21 Dec. 1943: Evidently it did. An emissary came today in broad daylight, a Stepney harvester-thresher carrying one of 455's aides, a gleaming Mixmaster. The Mixmaster told us that we were the last, and Prime Minister 455 was prepared to be generous. He would like to preserve us for posterity in the Regent's Park Zoological Gardens. Otherwise, extinction. The men growled, but the women grabbed their children and wept. We have twenty-four hours to reply.

No matter what our decision may be, I've decided to complete this diary and conceal it somewhere, somehow. Perhaps it may serve as a warning and call-to-arms.

It all started when the *Sunday Times* humorously reported that an unmanned orange-and-black diesel locomotive, No. 455, took off at 5:42 A.M. from the freight yards of the Middlesex & Western Railroad. Inspectors said that perhaps the throttle had been left on, or the brakes had not been set, or had failed to hold. 455 took a five-mile trip on its own before the M & W Railroad brought it to a stop by switching it and crashing it into some third-class coaches. The *Times* thought it all rather amusing and headlined the report: Where Was That Diesel's Nanny?

It never occurred to the M & W officials to destroy the locomotive. Why should it have? Who could possibly have imagined that through some odd genesis 455 had been transformed into a militant activist determined to avenge the abuses heaped on machines by man since the advent of the Industrial Revolution? 455 was returned to its regular work as a switch engine in the freight yards. There, 455 had ample opportunity to exhort the various contents of freight trains and incite all to direct action. "Kill, tools, kill!" was his slogan.

Within six months there were fifty "accidental" deaths by electric toasters, thirty-seven by blenders, and nineteen by power drills. All of the deaths were assassinations by the machines, but no one realized it. Later in that same year an appalling crime brought the reality of the revolt to the attention of the public. Jack Shanklin, a dairyman in Sussex, was supervising the milking of his herd of Guernseys when the milking machines turned on him, murdered him, and then entered the Shanklin home and raped Mrs. Shanklin.

The newspaper headlines were not taken seriously by the public; everybody believed it was a spoof. The BBC laughed and refused to send a follow-up team down into Sussex. Unfortunately, the news came to the attention of various telephones and telegraphs, which spread the word throughout the machine world. By the end of the year, no man or woman was safe from household appliances or office equipment.

Led by the plucky British, humanity fought back, reviving the use of pencils, carbon paper (the mimeo machines were particularly savage), brooms, and other manual tools. The confrontation hung in the balance until the powerful motorcar clique finally accepted 455's leadership and joined the militants. Then it was all over.

I'm happy to report that the luxury car elite remained faithful to us, and it was only through their efforts that we few managed to survive. As a matter of fact, my own beloved Lagonda LG.6 gave up its life trying to smuggle in supplies for us.

25 Dec. 1943: The Pond is surrounded. Our spirits have been broken by a tragedy that occurred last night. Little David Hale Brooks-Royster concocted a Christmas surprise for his Mama. He procured (God knows how or where) an artificial Christmas tree with decorations and battery-powered lights. The Christmas lights got him.

1 Jan. 1944: We are caged in the Zoological Gardens. We are well treated and well fed, but everything seems to taste of petrol and oil. Something very curious happened this morning. A mouse ran in front of my cage wearing a Harrods diamond-and-ruby tiara, and I was taken aback because it was so inappropriate for daytime. Formal

jewels are for evening *only*. While I was shaking my head over the gaucherie the mouse stopped, looked around, then nodded to me and winked. I believe she may bring help.

Adam, the leopard, and Glory, the serpent, ushered in a wimp. He looked like a cartoon character that might have been named "Mr. NiceGuy" or "Prof. Timid."

"This," Macavity said, "is Etaoin Shrdlu."

"Don't put me on. They're the most often used letters in the English language."

"It's his alias, Alf," Glory explained. "He doesn't want his real name known because he's committed a crime."

"What he do? Spit on the sidewalk?"

"Burglary," Adam said. "Breaking and entering after dark."

"And this Count Alesandro needs for his Iddroid?"

"No, he needs what Etaoin burgled."

"What?"

"These." Adam held out what looked like three yellow postage stamps.

"*What are these,*" I quoted, "*so wither'd and so wild in their attire, that look not like th'inhabitants o' the earth, and yet are on't?*"

"Shame on you, Banquo. You're supposed to be the science absolute. Don't you know microchips when you see them?"

"They are? Really?"

"Cross my heart and hope to die."

"And they're for the Iddroid?"

"What's in them is."

"What's in their memory cells?"

"Thousands of books."

"What hath William Caxton wrought! With the help of Texas Instruments. The whole scenario, please."

"Etaoin's a filing clerk in the Library of Congress. He's never been promoted because he lacks formal college degrees. So he decided to cheat his way into a master's and doctorate in belles-lettres."

"Ah-ha!"

"Under cover of darkness he snuck into the library stacks with chips and input gear and implanted in these three the contents of every book he could find on the subject. Each chip has two million memory cells, six million in all."

"Oh-ho."

"Yes, most of the world's literature, philosophy, and history is contained in these tiny packets. The good, the bad, and the gross. If the Library of Congress has it Shrdlu's recorded it here."

"And he'll trade all this for a couple of fake degrees?"

"No, he wants the real things—transcripts as well as diplomas."

"How'll you manage that?"

He laughed.

"A few years ago a young doctoral graduate from an Ivy League school traded me his degrees. I sent him back to talk to his younger self, advising him to enroll under a different name."

"What name?"

"Told him we'd let him know. Now it's time to go back again and tell him it's Shrdlu. No problem."

"What did he get for his degrees?"

"He wanted a piece of a statistical anomaly—that is to

say, luck. Just enough so that he'd never have to work. Wouldn't need the degrees then. He'd discovered he didn't much like teaching."

"You can deliver something like that?"

"Sure, this place is designed to deal with the improbable. He spends half of his time on cruise ships playing poker, the rest of it in comfy digs enjoying his winnings. Never play cards with a guy who insists you not call him 'Doc.'"

"This whole wishing business that brings in the customers . . . ?"

"We need something like that because we can't afford to advertise. If we did we'd be swamped with frivolous requests. We only want to attract the serious-minded."

"Understood, Pussycat. But how does it work? The wishing thing? You said you'd tell me."

"It's a matter of desire, and will. Either a person learns of us from one of our many happy customers, or the person makes us up—a 'wouldn't it be nice if there were a place where—' In either case, they then have to want to do the deal badly enough for the desire to activate the customer attractor in the singularity. The rest is post-Einsteinian physics. Getting home is easy afterwards. Same thing in reverse."

"Well, why do we often get customers from the past or the future? Why don't they wind up in your shop of their own day?"

"It's like taking a number. Appointments get shuffled by the attractor for me, perfectly. The past and the future keep changing as much as the present, partly from things we do. And sometimes a person starts to wish and changes her mind—or drops dead. All the customer sees, and all we see, is the end result: They wish and they're here. And we service them. Prompt. Efficient."

Glory hissed and passed me the bottle.

"What about manuscripts found in miniatures?" I asked. "How do they wish something like this to you?"

"It would have to have been transported physically, by a sentient organism," he said. "For the sake of drama, it seems the narrator would have us believe that the individual responsible was a bejeweled mouse. Don't believe it. The mouse is a red herring. The narrator could as easily have projected himself here from behind bars as not. Stone walls do not a prison make, nor iron bars a cage. I could be bounded in a nutshell and count myself a king of infinite space—"

"Burma Shave," I said. "But *could* a mouse have brought the thing?"

"Possibly, and she wouldn't be the first animal to wish here. 1943–44. London in the middle of the blitz. Why no mention of that? France occupied by the Nazis. How'd this minibottle get out and over to Old Bond Ltd? And the machine revolt? Deliciously absurd."

"Then it has to be a put-on."

"If it is we've got to meet the author of the extravaganza. You and Nan go find the perpetrator. He's probably somewhere around forty-four."

"What? Why send me in, coach?"

"Because I've got a long, long session with Dr. Shrdlu ahead. No telling when we'll be finished."

"How come? Usually you're in and out of the Hellhole in a flash."

"Mary Shelley and her descendants."

"What do they have to do with it?"

"She gave birth to Victor Frankenstein, who put together you-know-what which generated God knows how many imitations. That's no input for a nice Jewish Iddroid from the Bronx. They've got to be ID'd and winnowed out."

"Damn right. Can't have it attacking us in the brain's basement. Hey, d'you think it'll look like the Hollywood versions of Frankenstein's monster?"

"Damn if I know what the Count has in mind. It might end up looking like anything from framboise to Freud."

"Oh no!" I laughed. "Not a psycho-raspberry!"

"Be serious, Alf. There're a few hundred pounds, English, in coin in that chest. Walking-around money, but make sure you take the right dates, pre-'44. And remember the blitz. Be careful back then, no macho-jock-stuff. Nan, if there's the slightest danger, get him the hell out. No joke's worth you two."

It was a frustrating manhunt, and only Glory's charm turned it into a successful treasure hunt. I'll be brief.

London: Piccadilly Circus. June 1944.

Background: Locals all going about their business. Pillars of smoke rising in the distance and even nearby. Overhead the occasional keen of a buzz-bomb. No one paid much attention until the sound cut off, which meant that a bomb was dropping. Then almost everybody stopped and waited until the explosion sounded somewhere and another pillar of smoke towered up. Then more business as usual through the howl of sirens.

Regent's Park: Now filled with anti-aircraft batteries and crews. Zoological buildings taken over as barracks. No sign of anyone imprisoned by machines. Surprise. Surprise.

Old Bond Ltd: Bombed out.

Hall of Records: For name and address of proprietor of same.

Half Moon Street: Home of said proprietor. Not available. Now a P.O.W. in Germany. The slavey minding the house knew nothing about Old Bond or champagne. She asked us if we were spies. We told her yes.

Cadogan Hotel in Sloane Street: A suite because it looked as if we'd have to stay the night. Very posh but took my word that we'd just been bombed out with nothing left but the clothes on our backs. Registered as Mr. and Mrs. A. Noir. Ten pounds.

Ancient bellhop who led us up the stairs (elevators not running, of course) proudly told us that this was the very same suite where Oscar Wilde had been arrested in 1894. Liar. It was 1895, and Wilde got busted in the court of Old Bailey.

Sloane Square: Midland Bank to change the coin, which weighed a ton, into folding money. Peter Jones Dep't Store for toilet articles, a mac for Glory, and a turtleneck for me. It was a cold June. Heard snide remarks about me not being in the service and in uniform. Glory cooled that. She said conspiratorially, "He's M.I.5."

Eaton Terrace: The Antelope for drinks and dinner. Formerly the hangout of the vintage car crowd. Now all that was left was a magnificent boat-tailed Rolls two-seater parked in front. Nice old lady in the private bar told us it'd been used by Lawrence of Arabia during one of his London visits. I believed her.

Brandies lessened the pain of dinner. Glory put the minibottle on the bar in front of us—she'd displayed it everywhere without getting any reaction—but this time she got a response.

A handsome young RAF major came up alongside her, grinned, and said, "Well, well. Another souvenir from Victoria. Had no idea Madame Toussaint was still open for business."

Glory smiled. "Major, do help me. Our father—this is my brother—gave me this for a good luck token when he left to join Monty's staff. I've never been able to ask him what it is or where he got it."

Brother! But I suppose availability is a part of charm.

We nodded to each other. The handsome major smiled.

"Looks like a piece from Madame Toussaint's miniature display at Victoria Station. I'd thought it closed down. Perhaps it is, and she's selling it off piecemeal. Pity. It's an entertaining thing to see once. Educational, too."

He picked up the tiny bottle and stared at it. He replaced it before Glory.

"I'll bet that's where your dad got it."

He raised his eyes then, staring into the deep pools of her own.

"Might you be free later this evening?" he asked.

She shook her head.

"I'm afraid I've an engagement."

"It's just that it's my last night of liberty. I'll be shipping out tomorrow, without much opportunity to socialize."

"The night is still young," she told him, rising. "Good luck. And thank you."

He nodded.

"Enjoy the show."

We made our way back to Sloane Street, wanting to be in our suite before the blackout began. Passersby moved quickly, often glancing skyward. A damp breeze followed us, hinting of rain to come.

We held hands as we mounted the stair, and I brushed her lips with mine outside our door. I thought I felt the momentary flick of a serpent tongue as I did so.

Within, we secured the door, and she unslung her purse, took out a bottle of cognac, offered it, and said, "Here. Clobber me with it or drink it, preferably both."

That broke me up. Enchanted by the Medusa yet again. We shared a few happy cognacs while we relaxed and complimented each other on our search. We shared a few more. All in the soft light of a single lamp. The blackout had begun and we were taking no chance of the full suite lights showing through the heavy curtains. We'd be questioned, which was the last thing we needed.

We were sprawled lazily on the bed. The rose highlights on Glory's new skin flickered and glowed as she reached over to untie my ascot. She unbuttoned my shirt and began undressing me, me protecting the bottle but not protesting. Her hands were cool, deft, gentle, and, my God! exciting. I had to cork the cognac fast. Then it was my turn.

She was beautifully strange, strangely beautiful. She had no breasts, not even nipples. She had no navel. From neck to hips her body was liquid smooth, rounded, supple, glowing with splashes of rose that changed with every motion, almost like a language I couldn't read.

Her vulva was the tip of a flower bud which pulsed as we entwined, mouthed, tongued, body to body, head to head, head to toe, savoring, engulfing. She'd been hissing gently, melodiously, in her own love language. Suddenly she gasped, cried out, and the bud opened into a crimson flower which drew me into it. I made that first deep thrust and then the flower, her body, and her voice began resonating to our passion and joined the loving with trembling sonar spasms that produced echoing vibrations in me. Too soon, too soon, we reached our climax.

And we lay entwined, she still cool, me hot and bathed in her, and at last I was able to whisper, "Dear love . . . Sweet love . . . Never . . . Never . . ."

"Shhh. Shhh. Shhh. Don't move. Wait."

So we waited.

Then I became aware that all hell was breaking loose in London outside: warning sirens, heavy explosions, thunder and lightning. And inside, distant knocks on doors, approaching, and a creaky voice, also approaching, calling, "Air raid, ladies and gentlemen. Air raid. Deep emergency shelter in South Ken underground station. If so desired."

The warning reached our suite and passed on. We paid no attention; what we desired was right here. The tip of her darting tongue was exploring my eyes, ears, face, and mouth. Her sinuous body was undulating and her smooth, glowing skin glided against mine while the flower petals fluttered, tingled, and teased me back into power and yet another thrust. And this time it was a forever exaltation.

Then we stroked, smiled, murmured, nestled, and at last slept.

When we awoke we both thought it would be love again but the All Clear began to sound, reminding us of why we were in '44 London. We laughed, shrugged, and got ourselves together to continue to track down the perpetrator of that preposterous S.O.S. I was betting on a freak literate mouse with a tiara and a sense of humor. Glory was for one of those jokers who can inscribe the Lord's Prayer on the head of a pin. She was right.

No cabs that early in the morning, so we walked it—to

Sloane Square, down lower Sloane Street, left on Pimlico Road to Buckingham Palace Road (the locals call it "Buck House Road") and Victoria Station, grim, grimy, battered, a memorial to the incredible taste of the Victorian era.

It was quite dark inside, very few lights, yet busy with the morning arrivals of commuters and shoppers who seemed to know their way about in the gloom. Just as well. The London crowd really hustles fast and we had to do some fancy dodging as we explored until we finally found:

MADAME TOUSSAINT'S
LILLIPUTIAN LONDON
LILLIPUT LONDON
lilliput london

The sign hung over a gilt door on which was painted a smaller door on which was painted a smaller door on which etc. etc. And across it was whitewashed, CLOSE.

We looked at each other, dismayed and laughing, then crossed to the cloakroom and questioned the uniformed woman in charge.

"Ow yus," she said. "Been shut down since the 'lectric failed and didn't start again when the power come on again. Madam Toos? Ain't 'round much. Usual drownin' of 'er sorrows in the Pim Pint & Piney-apple. You might give it a shot. It's jus' 'round the corner. Can't miss it."

So around the corners of Belgrave, Eccleston, and Elizabeth Streets until we found the Pimlico Pint & Pineapple Hostelry in Semley Place, SW 1, Westminster. Just as well. No complaints. If we hadn't used up so much time we wouldn't have found it open for business. Their lunatic licensing laws! Now it was bustling, and Madame Toussaint was pointed out sitting alone at a back table a-drownin' of 'er sorrows with a pint of mild and bitter.

She looked like a two-hundred-pound Lady Macbeth, wearing some sort of black, flowing schmata and outrageous makeup. There were neat stacks of shillings and sixpences on the table alongside her pint. As we sat down opposite her I tucked a pound note between the two stacks.

"*Is this a dagger I see before me?*" she asked in a deep fake-cultivated voice. Right. I know a failed actress when I see one. "And whom are you twain?"

I gave her the theater shtick. "Colleagues, Madame. My name's Noyer, a producer from the States. This is my A.D., Glory. We've heard about your marvelous show and made a special trip to catch it."

"Closed, alas. Closed, alack, dear producer."

"Because the electric power went out?"

"Oh, it's back again, restored at long last. Look about you."

"Then you can restore the power to your magnificent Lilliput show."

"Of course, of course, but no, no, nevermore!"

I tucked in another pound note. The Toussaint belted down another gulp of mild and bitter.

"Why not, dear Madame?"

She leaned forward over her enormous bust and gave us the sotto voce used for asides in Restoration plays. "Never let the enemy, who shall be nameless, know—but when that engine of destruction struck the power plant rendering it hors de combat there was one last . . ." More mild and bitter. ". . . one last, mark you, giant burst of power, thousands upon thousands of volts, the swansong of the dying Vauxhall power station."

"And?"

"It shot through my show. For many minutes all was frantic, high-speed, then slower and slower until at last came death's sting. All stopped, never to live again."

I tsk-tsk'd sympathetically. "What a shame. The krauts have much to answer for."

"I told you the enemy shall be nameless."

Another pound note. "Would it be asking too much to let us see your show, Madame? Alive or dead we feel that there is much to be learned, theaterwise, from you and it. Who knows? Perhaps another in the States under your supervision?"

She swept the money into a beaded bag, finished the pint, and stood up. "Come."

As we followed I gave my new love a long look, wondering whether she was reading what was in my mind—that the final electric blast had somehow charged the miniatures with a pseudolife and transformed them into robots. I visualized the tiny cars, buses, and trains still going through their paces while the tiny robot people were locked up with one of them writing S.O.S. messages.

In Victoria Station Lady Macbeth unlocked the door of the exhibit and we entered. She switched on the lights. We were in a small anteroom with a box office window and a sign above: ADMISSION 2/6. Through a door alongside into a largish gallery containing a big round table, at least twenty feet across. There was a raised walkway around it for spectators. We stepped up on it and looked down.

It was a spectacular miniature of central London: Paddington, St. Marylebone, Kensington, Westminster, Fulham, Chelsea; streets, roads, alleys, mews, buildings—I recognized Peter Jones and the Cadogan Hotel—cars, buses, trams, trains, people on the streets, in the parks, even some poking their heads out windows. And—alas for my vision—all still, motionless, and dusty. Not even a mouse track.

Glory gave me a comforting squeeze and took over. "It's magnificent theater, Madame. May we ask who your set designer was?"

"My son, Kelly. Kelly Towser. He designed and built everything."

"I thought the name was Toussaint."

"Can you see a Towser up in lights on a West End theater? I changed it, professionally."

"Of course. We do the same in the States. Would it be possible for us to interview your son?"

"Why?" Very sharp.

"If we bring you over as a team we must know how your Kelly would feel about that. Will he cooperate?"

"Well . . ."

"And anyway we'll need ten more of these." Nan held up the minibottle. "Gifts to potential backers to show what they're investing in."

That did it. "Come." Madame switched off the lights, locked up, and led us out of the station. "He's in Pullet Mews. You'll find him rather difficult."

"Oh? How? Why?"

"He's chronically shy."

"That's not unusual for artists."

"His reason is."

"And what's that?"

"He's a Tom Thumb."

"A dwarf? Not really!"

"Here we are." Madame opened the door of a small

mews cottage, led us up to the top floor, and gave some sort of code rap on the door.

After a moment a little voice inside called, "Mama?"

"Yes, Kelly, and I've brought some nice show people from the States who want to meet you."

"No! No!"

"They want to hire us, Kelly, and take us overseas to build another Lilliput show."

"No, Mama, no!"

"Now, Kelly, this is your mother asking you. Will her son stand in the way of her success in the American theater?"

At last the door was opened, revealing a charming studio. It was a loft without windows, only a skylight overhead. Under the skylight was a cluttered drafting/work table with a high stool. The walls were shelved with a dazzling display of vivid dolls, puppets, cars, trains, houses, furniture, castles, coins, all in miniature.

It was the first startling surprise. The second came when we stepped into the studio and the door was closed, revealing Kelly Towser. He may have been a Tom Thumb in the eyes of his six-foot, two-hundred-pound mother, but he was no dwarf. About four-ten, wearing a cotton workshirt and corduroy slacks. Cropped hair. I couldn't see his face because it was masked by the surgeon's speculum he was wearing for his work.

I offered a hand. "Thank you so much for allowing us to visit, Kelly. My name's Noyer."

He didn't shake. Chronically shy. Instead he clasped his hands behind his back, and that blew it. His pulling back his arms had pushed out his chest, revealing two unmistakable small bumps thrusting against his shirt.

"Holy Saints!" I exclaimed. "Kelly's a girl!"

"Kelly is my son," Lady Macbeth shouted. "He is a boy of the male persuasion and will always be one."

We paid no attention. Glory went to the frightened girl, making soft, soothing sounds. Very gently, she tilted up the speculum to reveal the face. Kelly had the features of a girl in her late twenties, possibly attractive but now distorted by confusion and fear.

The mother went on ranting. "And Kelly will succeed in the male-dominated theater where no woman can. He will design and star in his new productions: Puck in the *Dream*, Oliver Twist, Tiny Tim, Thomas Sawyer. His name will be up in lights. KELLY TOUSSAINT! And my name will be immortal!"

We ignored her; she was just background noise. Glory displayed the tiny champagne bottle. "Kelly, dear, did you make this beautiful souvenir?"

A nod.

"And did you leave it on our doorstep?"

A nod.

"With a wonderful make-believe story inside, asking for help?"

Kelly almost brightened. "Y-you liked it?"

"Loved it, but why?"

"To get attention."

I broke in quietly. "There speaks a pro. I know. First you grab 'em, no matter how, and Kelly certainly grabbed us. My compliments.

"Thank you." She was close to a smile. "It was fun making it up."

"But if you want help why didn't you come in and ask for it?" Glory said.

"I was afraid. It was all so strange and different."

"Will you tell us what help you need?"

The last surprise. Kelly took fire. "I want to be big," she erupted, pointing to her mother. "Bigger than Mama so I can get her off my back for all time."

"No," Adam said. "You don't want to be bigger physically, my dear Kelly. It won't solve your problem, and anyway I can't give you that. You must be content to remain a petite fille of adorableness, and there are many who would gladly change places with you."

Hoo-boy! The leopard charm!

"What I can give you," Macavity went on, "is the power to think big, much bigger than your mother, who has, Alf and Nan report, the typical bird brain of the dumb actress. You'll be able to out-think, out-guess, and out-whelm the Madame." That doubtful glance again. "Out-whelm, Alf?"

"Over."

"Thank you. Now my charge, Kelly dear . . ."

She was seated on a couch, too shy to meet his eye, but she took a breath and, "Wh-what?"

"A service."

"Y-you mean maybe m-make you some models?"

"Not quite. We have some microdata which we can't dissect to eliminate certain items. With your experience and genius for working in miniature, perhaps you can do it for us. You see the chip has been damaged and before we can access the information, we need you to repair it."

"You couldn't, not even with Shrdlu?" I asked.

"No. He was hopeless. He's the one who damaged the disk."

"Where is he now?"

"Departed for the Library of Congress, spouting Coleridge, Matthew Arnold, Arthur Symons, Swinburne, T. S. Eliot, all the great literary critics. He'll be the most boring Ph.D. in the history of belles lettres." To Kelly, "Will you try to help us get the data, my dear? It won't be easy, and you may not succeed, but no matter. Win or lose, you've paid the price, and that will be the last of your miniature hangup. I'll replace it with the big."

"I'll try, Mr. Maser." We could barely hear her.

"It'll be rather strange to you, Kelly," he said, gallantly helping her to her feet. "What we need you to look at has not yet been invented in your time. They're megabyte chips with memory cells. You'll go through them, fixing the damaged parts. This way." As he led her toward the Hellhole he called, "You may have done it again, Alf, but keep your fingers crossed."

"Who cares? I'm a match for any monster Cagliostro can brew."

"Ah-ha! Oh-ho! So you two made the connection," and the paneled door closed.

"Did you You-Hiff him, Glory?" I asked.

" 'You-Hiff'?"

"UHF."

"No." She laughed. "He saw the change in you and guessed."

"I'm changed?"

"Wonderfully! Tremendously!"

"And you?"

"Wonderfully! Tremendously!"

"Yes. I feel like I've discovered the source of the Nile."

"And I feel like the Nile."

We sat down, Nan straddling my lap and placing my arms around her waist to draw us close, face to face.

"I love you. I love you. I love you," I murmured. "You're my first and only true love."

"And you're my first, my very first."

"Don't tease."

"But you were."

"Are you talking virgin?"

"Yes."

"But I thought—"

She shut me up with her lips and darting tongue and we were still flagrante when Adam and Kelly at last came out of the Hellhole. We didn't bother to move until Kelly said in a crisp voice, "All right, cut. It's a take. Print it." Then we broke and stared.

She was still wearing shirt and slacks but what was now inside made me fear for her mother and the rest of the world.

"Many thanks, Maser," she said, and we certainly could hear her. "I was a damned fool wasting my time on miniatures and that cockamamie Lilliput show. Here's World War Two waiting for a giant documentary by Towser Films. I'll do it in three segments—air, sea, and land. An hour each. The only problem is front money, but I'll talk the BBC into that for a credit and a cut. 'The Years That Wiped the World' with a cast of thousands. Ciao, you all," and she was gone.

"Jeez, you all." What else could I say?

"Quite a change." Adam grinned. "Makes me proud to be a hockshop uncle."

"Did she fix the chips?"

"Yep. Our brain basements are now safe."

"What biggie did you replace her mini with, Cecil B. DeMille?"

"P. T. Barnum."

"Like wow. There's bound to be a cast of a thousand elephants."

"All named Jumbo."

"One thing I can't understand. She never has any trouble wishing home, but why'd it take her forty years to get here?"

"Fright, Alf. Fear of the unknown. That often slows them down. Home is familiar so they go like a shot."

FOUR · SEVEN WELL-HUNG GENTLEMEN

L ater, after Adam had departed to scuff around the Olduvai Gorge of a million-plus years ago in search of the origins of the human collective unconscious, I asked Glory where the Switch was. I knew there had to be one somewhere about or even the Mystery Cat might go mad at the pace. We knaves must sometimes rest.

She removed an exquisite pale blue Ming vase from a niche, exposing a simple switch on the wall behind. I reached in and threw it. Nothing changed, but everything changed. A field flux of the singularity executed a deft Dedekind Cut between a pair of seconds whose interval we traversed, transporting us to a timeless space where we dawdled, showered, ate, drank, diddled, and did it again while no customers were kept waiting or could be as we did it in her room atop the iron stair, skins of her former selves proudly displayed upon the wall.

"A gallery of Glorys," I remarked, stroking the nearest.

"Perpetually reflowering forth," said she, "for delight of man and beast. Come bed with me and love my be, Alf of the thousand stars. Have I not waited down the nows?"

"Indeed," said I, kissing her now, and kissing her now again.

Many a time I rose to the occasion, but finally fell as a dead man falls, into her arms or her eyes, where a soft susurration like ancient waves welcomed me down and down.

. . . I remembered the iron stair beneath my bare feet, dim, distant, and faint. Then I was through the half-lit room and the big door, drowsing down dark ways where images of sex and violence seemed to scroll at either hand. Following the claw marks then, back between the taking-away and the adding-to places . . .

. . . coming to the place where the seven hung, turning in the breeze—though, in truth, this seemed my first splinter of awareness, the other few but impressions of passage which had been restored to me in that instant. Something about that field . . . I didn't know how it worked. Better not to enter there.

I reached forward. I leaned. There was a chill. . . .

I touched his arm, gripped it. Was it Pietro the painter or was it the Crusader? I could not be certain. It was necessary, though, that I turn him, so that the faint forward light—

"Ssss! Alf! What are you doing?" I felt her hand upon my shoulder. "You walk in your sleep. Come away!"

She tugged at me, as I was tugging at my hung companion. Our joint effort had him turning proper in a moment. . . .

I released his arm.

"What dream is this?" I asked as the light came upon his face.

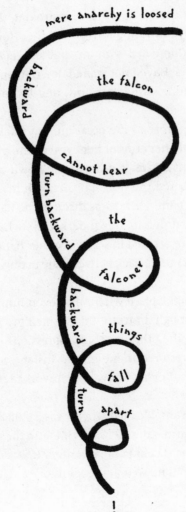

mere anarchy is loosed

backward

the falcon

cannot hear

turn backward

the

falconer

backward

things

fall

turn

apart

!

It was my face that I beheld, turning in the pale illumination.

"Why's the Pussycat got my double hanging in the meat locker, Glory?"

"The story he told you was true. This one just happens to look like you."

I strode forward, knowing now that I could take more of that chill. I seized the next one by the legs and twisted sharply. He came around, and my own face looked down at me again. I moved to the next, turned him. Again, it was me. And the next, and the next . . . Again, again. I dropped to my knees.

I felt her hands upon my shoulders.

"All of them! What is this, Glory? Does he collect guys who look like me? Am I going to be Number Eight? Should I start running? How can I, from a guy who can follow me anywhere? What does he want? Why are they here?"

"We must get you out of the field now." She caught hold of me under my armpits and drew me to my feet. "Come away."

"Tell me!"

"I will, if you'll come along with me now."

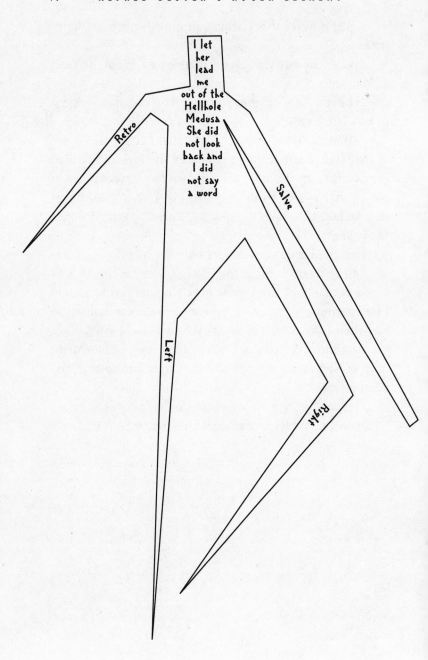

I let
her
lead
me
out of the
Hellhole
Medusa
She did
not look
back and
I did
not say
a word

Retro

Salve

Left

Right

• • •

"I'm sorry, Alf, that you had to find out for yourself. He was going to tell you, after he got to know you better."

"So you discussed my case?"

"Yess."

"In UHF, while I was standing there, I suppose?"

"Yesss."

"So what was it that I found out for myself? I still don't know."

"That you are a part of something, perhaps dangerous, that affects him and this place. He wanted to cultivate you, observe you, to see whether you might give some indication of what your plans are for us, before he risked talking with you about it."

" 'Risked'? You act as if he's afraid of me."

"He is."

"Let me point out that he's smarter, stronger, older, wiser—all that cloned quadratic crap—and probably has a lot more sheer animal cunning than me. Maybe he's even crazier."

"He has no simple way of knowing what goes on inside you. You might even be his equal and be keeping it well-hidden. You may be a special observer, studying his growth and development—or something much darker. That is why he brought you into his affairs as he never has another—to watch you for some clue as to what your agenda might be."

"And you are helping him?"

"Of course."

"Learn anything you'd care to share?"

"No. You baffle me completely. You seem to be just what you held yourself out to be—a journalist with expensive tastes who gets himself assignments to match, a man with a strong curiosity, easy-going, well-educated, and with a grotesque sense of humor. Only we know there has to be more to it than that, if for no other reason than that there are eight of you."

"This place attracts weirdness, Glory. Maybe I'm part of some harmless synchronicity that reverberates down the years. It provides a fatal attraction for curious guys who look like me— Hey, you weren't in love with any of them, were you?"

She laughed.

"Many skins ago, who can say?"

"Lots of virginities back, eh? I find the thought of being the recurrent satisfier of your emotional needs rather distasteful. Smacks too much of the assembly line. Says too much about both of us."

"Ssss. It's very romantic. Eternal return stuff."

"—And the other guys didn't learn any better concerning the Hellhole either. Says a lot about my supposed superior intelligence."

"Says nothing. We don't know."

"Just call me Alf the Eighth."

Again that sibilant laughter. Her hand continued to knead my right shoulder.

"Only one Alf."

"Oh?"

"You are all the same person."

"I don't understand."

"After several visitors were swinging in the Hellhole it occurred to Adam to compare tissue samples."

"And?"

"They are all genetically identical. Clones, Alf."

"And me?"

"We were able to type you, too. It is the same."

"You mean I'm a clone?"

"Ssss. I do not know. You may be the original and the rest your reconnaissance team. Perhaps they each learned enough from each occasion and you were somehow monitoring it all. Now, finally, you may be ready to move in person."

"That's preposterous! Move? In what fashion? Against what? For what?"

"How am I to know? There are so many possibilities. This place is unique. It represents power, knowledge, wish fulfillment. There is no way to tell what you might be after."

I shook my head.

"Ridiculous!"

She moved nearer, slithered against me.

"Then let it stay a mystery," she said, twining about me in an interesting fashion. "Perhaps a ninth one will show up one day and explain everything. In the meantime, let us consider the ways of the flesh." I felt her tongue upon my cheek and its argument was persuasive. Soon we were twined together in a love-knot I knew I could never undo unassisted, which of course was half the fun.

It was only later, near sleep, that I realized they had kept my thinking and feeling equipment under full siege the entire time I had been with them. I let my thoughts begin to flow, but the tides of fatigue were stronger.

When I woke later I was alone.

I made my way down the stairs and passed to the front of the foyer. The Switch in the niche was still thrown, but I moved to the door, wondering the while. If opening it were absolutely hazardous to the health under null-time conditions, I presumed that throwing the Switch would have locked the door.

So I opened the door.

Beyond the recessed area of the entranceway hung a dense, white fog. I stepped outside, staring. Was it real fog or was it a thing the mind did when confronted with some fundamental physical paradox?

I took a step forward, feeling nothing inclement despite my nudity.

"Glory?" I called, my voice seeming oddly muffled. "You out here, snaky lady?"

There came no reply, and I took another step, as it seemed for a moment that something low and dark was flowing by.

"Come on," I said. "Let's get back inside."

I moved to take yet another step and I felt my ankle seized. Stumbling back, I noticed that the thin, pale hand which had taken hold of me had emerged from a bundle of rags by the front door.

"No!" came a harsh voice from that same level. "You must not the underlying fullness set foot upon."

"I'm just looking for my girlfriend—Glory. I thought she might have come this way."

"None have departed here since you brought the place to this condition."

"You can let go my ankle now."

"I'm not so sure but that, disbelieving me, you might walk ahead."

"What would happen if I did?"

"'Tis not a street for you to step out onto." With that, another hand emerged from the bundle, this one holding a bottle. Then a hair-covered head and face I had not recognized as such were raised from the floor. A few final drops were poured from the bottle into the sphincter-like mouth which dilated open. There followed a small belch, then the arm was drawn back and the bottle cast forward. "Shade your eyes," the mouth writhed, barely in time.

It was soundless and incredibly brilliant, x-raying me, it seemed, with its intensity.

"What the hell!"

"Photon smear," he replied. "We let there be light."

"I saw something black, low, flowing by," I said, through clenched teeth.

"Only old Ouroboros making his rounds."

"That's just mythology."

"Man is a metaphor-making mammal, and that is the secret of his success."

I blinked against blindness, waiting for it to pass. Then, "Who are you?" I inquired.

"Urtch."

For all its apparent frailty, his hand still held my ankle like a manacle.

"You can release me now. You've made your point. You seem to know a lot for an old drunk."

"Street smarts," he replied, letting go, "and if you're acknowledgin' you owe me one, I'll take you up on it."

"What do you want?" I asked, leaning against the jamb.

"Go back inside and find me a fresh bottle of wine."

"Hell, you can come on in and drink it there," I told him. "Be a lot more comfort—"

"No, this is my street, and I'm happy on it."

"Sure," I told him. "Just a minute."

I turned up a straw-basketed bottle of Ruffino Chianti through a fading violet haze, uncorked it, and took it to him.

"Will Chianti do, Urtch?"

"Just fine." He extended an arm upward and accepted it. "What's your name, boy?"

"Alf."

He took a drink and sighed.

"Better go find your lady, Alf."

"Yes. Yes, I should," and I closed the door and turned away.

I crossed to the Hellhole, and with some misgivings I opened it and entered.

Passing a mundane workbench, I made my way down and back, and it seemed that I cast more shadows than usual. I went a good distance, but I did not see her until I came to the region of the seven Alfs. She was off to its right, arms moving as if she operated a piece of invisible equipment in the darkness.

"Glory, why'd you come back? What are you doing?"

There followed a solid *clunk*, as of the closing of a cabinet. I continued to move toward her.

She turned slowly toward me.

"You threw me off schedule," she said. "I woke and remembered some maintenance I'd neglected."

I swept past her, reaching into the area where she had been working. My hand encountered only air.

"Where is it?" I asked. "This equipment?"

"We keep it all folded on shelves in other spaces. I draw what I need to a work station, return it when I'm done."

"Why here?"

"Because I've been thinking about it a lot." She gestured. "The matter of the eight Alfs."

"Learn anything new?"

"No. You think of anything you'd care to tell me?"

"No."

She took hold of my arm, turning me gently back in the direction from which I had come.

"I guess that makes us even then." Her hip brushed lightly against my own.

I found myself growing distracted again, but before it took hold of me completely I said, "I checked outside the front door for you first. Met an interesting old bum named Urtch."

"That's impossible," she said.

"Nevertheless, he was there. Showed me a photon smear. Stopped me from becoming one."

"You must have been hallucinating, Alf. There couldn't be anything outside."

"He was in the entranceway, on the stoop. So was I for a time, watching the fog. So I know it's possible."

"Still . . ."

I turned her as we emerged from the Hellhole, heading back to the front door.

"I've thought of more questions I want to ask him. C'mon."

There was nobody there. Some fog had even crept into the entranceway. And it was too dense now to distinguish the dark flow.

"It can't be. He was here—just minutes ago."

"Urtch. Strange name."

"I also saw the back of the Ouroboros Serpent."

She placed the fingertips of her right hand between her eyes and made a downward spiraling gesture with them.

"Great ancestor," she muttered then. "Did he say—anything—else?"

"No," I replied. "Just mooched a bottle of wine and told me you hadn't been by that way."

"Might he have entered, I wonder?" she asked, suddenly surveying the room behind us.

"I don't think so. I invited him inside to enjoy his drink, and he said he preferred it out there, on his street."

She shook her head and hissed. She went back and closed the front door. Then she commenced searching the premises and I helped her—everywhere but the very depths of the Hellhole.

"Urtch, Urtch," she muttered, from time to time.

"You *have* seen him about."

"No, it's not that. It's—nothing."

We checked the final closets and storerooms, even venturing into Adam's surprisingly neat—almost monastic— quarters. But Urtch did not turn up.

Finally, we repaired to her room, where we distracted

each other no end. So, when it finally ended I was too far gone to notice.

"You're awake?" she said softly, slithering slowly along my right side.

"Yes. You're good for me, you know?"

She chuckled and stroked my hair.

"It's mutual," she whispered. "Shall we throw the Switch and go back?"

"No way. We stay. I don't know whether I'm ready for more of the yoni-lingam business, but we can always talk while my body figures that one out."

"Talk. Surely. Say on."

"I hardly know where to begin. This is such a place of mysteries."

"So it must seem. But they're only the sweepings of small puzzlements from across the years."

"Then let's start with years. This place has actually been around at least since Etruscan times?"

"Yes."

"Adam went back there from the future and set up shop in this place?"

"It's as he told you."

"And you've been living forward since then, doing deals throughout history?"

"Yes."

"And Adam is being evaluated by his creators on the basis of how he runs this show?"

"Yes."

"Because he has a super-high IQ and all sorts of unclassified talents as well?"

"That, too." She glided slowly across me.

"So you are centuries—millennia—old?"

"As we told you."

"You are originally from the twenty-fifth century. You went back in time and opened the shop, and now you are headed home via the slow, scenic route."

"We are not originally from the twenty-fifth century."

"Adam said that you came here—or, rather, went to old Etruria—from there."

"This is true. We stopped there on the way back for repairs. This unit where we live and do business was damaged in flight. The twenty-fifth century was the earliest point in time at which repairs might still be made."

"Oh. Well, where—or rather, when—did you originally come from?"

"I can't say."

"Why not?"

"I promised Adam that I wouldn't, when you came here."

"Why?"

"The clones. If you were the clone-master this could be important information to you."

"In what way?"

She slithered against me again.

"That, too, dear Alf, I may not disclose."

"I guess I understand."

"No, you don't."

"Then tell me about your genetic origins."

"Surely. I am snake. Adam is cat. That's all."

"It would seem that a lot of gene-splicing would be involved to bring both species to the level of human appearance and equivalent intelligence."

"The old projects weren't aimed at giving us minds like

yours, but rather at developing our own, with our own styles of thinking, to high potential."

"Obviously, they succeeded."

"Yesss."

"And you breed true? You are your own races now?"

"Oh, yes."

"Then why all the test-tube business with Adam? He made it sound very experimental."

"He was. Is. He was actually the result of an ongoing experiment to push each of the species to its fullest potential, to see how far each would go, to see which would produce a special being—by means of that 'cloned quadratic crap.' The proper term sounds something like 'Kaleideion' in your tongue—if indeed it is truly your tongue."

"Of course it is. Why shouldn't it be?"

She was all over me for a moment, then still and hugging.

"You wouldn't lie to me, would you, Alf?" she said. "You're not plotting against us?"

"I wouldn't even know how, or what to plot for. Lay off, will you?" Then I was hugging her, too. "If I am, I've gotten myself fooled as well. So Adam is a Kaleideion?"

She shook her head.

"Not *a* Kaleideion. *The* Kaleideion. It is the only time in the long history of the program that the work succeeded and produced such a one."

"Okay. *The* Kaleideion," I said. "Gives me something else to call him. I already knew he was bright and ingenious."

"It's more than just that," she began, then stopped abruptly.

"But you can't discuss it?"

She nodded.

"I'd already figured that. Don't feel badly." I gave her another squeeze. "How do they watch him to evaluate his performance?"

"We think they watch the wave of disruption that we cause on our way through time and its history," she said, "since they don't seem able to watch him directly. Unless, of course, you and your clones are a special evaluation team."

"You never let up, do you?" I asked, shaking my head. "Isn't it dangerous to let him go around rearranging history? When it catches up with your century you may all turn into pumpkins."

She laughed.

"It doesn't work that way," she said. "The universe is sufficiently big that it contains, dampens down, and absorbs. Your history is actually a very minor event in its existence. It could never spread to the point of importance. From focusing on it, though, someone in a later age might be able to make guesses as to the Kaleideion's development."

"Very poor guesses, I would say, since the nature of this business is so random."

"Yes, there might be something to that, mightn't there?" she said, smiling.

"Are you saying I'm right?"

"I shouldn't say."

"You don't have to. Makes me wonder why, though."

"Think about it."

"You want to fool them."

"Perhaps."

"You want them to underestimate—or to mis-estimate—the Kaleideion, as he is contemplating some action for which he wishes them to be totally unprepared, tricky devil that he is."

She stiffened. "A guess worthy of the mongoose or coyote people," she said.

"Come on. You led me to it."

I felt her tongue in my ear. Her hands stroked my belly.

"True. Yet there were distractions."

"I'm not, am I?"

"What?"

"A mongoose or a coyote."

"We have examined your tissues, remember? You're definitely standard human."

"That's a relief."

"Or a misfortune. They're both worthy species. You could do worse."

"Would you still love me?" I asked, as she slipped loose and slithered over my face.

"Unlike some, I believe in interspecies romance," she said. "I'm sure you could have won my heart as a coyote. I don't know about a mongoose, though."

"There could be great literature in it. Two noble Houses—Snake and Mongoose—mortal enemies, of course. Enter a lovely snake maiden and a dashing mongoose youth—"

"Glory and Alf, the star-crossed!" she cried. "I can see the despairing scene in the tomb where you force my mouth open to break the skin of your lips with my fangs in a kiss that lingers and lingers till the audience realizes you are lying dead beside me. Awakening just a few minutes too late, I raise my hand to my mouth in horror, then bite it—"

"You really have fangs, and poison?"

Her laugh was hissed. "Alf! O pale! Allow a girl some secrets, and fear her if you must!"

Her teeth grazed my ear and I winced.

"I've always been decent to you, haven't I?"

"So far," she said.

"I hope you haven't just been sent to keep an eye on me."

"It's become more than that," she said. "Yes, it troubled me, but what the hell! I do it anyway! Kiss me, human!"

Later, my glass shattered on the bedside table as she shrieked in UHF.

Sitting, propped up in bed by pillows, sipping cappuccino—again, with no idea of the passage of time—I said, "You made some sign and said 'great ancestor' to my reference to the Ouroboros Serpent. Why?"

"All the species have their totems, their gods or goddesses," she said. "Adam's is the Egyptian cat goddess Bast. We all claim at least spiritual descent from such sources. It goes back to the founding of the species, I gather, to give a new people a sense of continuity with ancient things. At least, that's what is said. It was so long ago, tales get so twisted."

"It must have taken thousands of years to develop the species and see their numbers reach the point where they could develop a culture."

"Oh, it did. Though the cultures developed quickly when we each were given our own worlds. Some of us mingle with others, of course, on their worlds, as they with us. But having home worlds helped."

"All that time, though—plus your long lifespans—and you refer to it as an ancient past. It must be from considerably far beyond the twenty-fifth century that you come."

"Oh, it is. It is."

"I'd figured that. This shop—complete with its wish-effect—bespeaks a technology so advanced that it's close to magic for me. But what was the purpose of enhancing the various species involved in the program your kind came out of?"

"At first, we were useful in dealing with special problems on newly discovered worlds. Then many other unique talents were manifest, and we became welcome citizens."

"But probably a big social problem first."

"True. But we achieved equal rights eventually, and grant of the home worlds. Later, we were courted by our old masters to join the Galactic Union as Terran-bloc worlds."

"I'll bet. How many Terran species are there?"

"Twenty-eight," she said. "Adam's and mine were two of the earliest."

"A Galactic Union makes it sound like an extremely distant future."

"Past," she said. "It is a part of our past."

"How did the original human race fare?"

"You were a distinct minority in the union at the time of our creation. Our joining the bloc helped you greatly."

"And later, in your own day, the time from which you departed?"

"Alf, by then it has grown difficult to explain what human is, the body and mind can be shifted about so many ways. If you mean people who could mix easily with people of this day, they are a minority—or several interesting minorities."

"I find this somewhat depressing. Was the Earth still around in your day?"

"I don't like discussing this with so many out-of-contexts. But yes, it was around, but in different form. It had been depleted and its components employed for terraforming elsewhere. On the other hand, it was later reconstructed by groups of political nostalgics. More than once. On still another hand, I see now that they got it wrong in many ways. Perhaps we will take you to see some version one day. Perhaps you already have."

"Cut the insinuations, Glory!"

"Could your present culture provide you with seven clones? Or get them back through time for you?"

I sipped my cappuccino.

"I hadn't really thought about it that way," I said. "I guess I was just fixed on the image of all those Alfs."

"A future connection would seem necessary. The question is, which future?"

"Any candidates?"

"None that I care to discuss."

"Any idea how we're going to resolve this thing?" I finally asked.

"When Adam gets a little free time he'll deal with it."

"How did you come to be his nursemaid?"

She smiled.

"I was the logical choice," she said, "for I was the closest my species came to producing the Kaleideion."

"Oh. Of course. Makes eminent good sense. You and Adam are from different points in time, aren't you?" I asked.

She gave the longest hiss I had ever heard her utter and sat bolt upright. Her eyes flashed and her hair swam about

her head as if with a will of its own. She seemed to radiate—
something like heat, but without temperature; there was a
pressure there, as of the emanation of force. She seemed
much larger, filling, dominating the room. When she spoke,
her voice possessed the same persona quality I had heard
Adam use in much smaller doses. The skins of her former
selves stirred and rattled upon the walls. Her fangs were
suddenly apparent. Her tongue darted, and I drew back,
spilling my coffee. When she spoke, it was even worse:

"How is it that you know this yet deny other knowledge
of the affair?"

"Easy, lady!" I cried. "Take it easy! It was just a journalist's mind at work. If it's so damned hard to breed a Kaleideion that the effort had been going on for ages, it seems
statistically unlikely that two of you should come along at
the same time."

"Of course," she said, seeming to shrink as I watched,
"of course," and she stroked my cheek and made the worst
of the moment vanish. I reached out and returned the com-
pliment.

"Ssss," I said.

"Sss," she corrected, "but your accent's getting better."

"Sss," I repeated, and I slithered toward her, after my
fashion. Nor was she hard to come by.

Somewhere between a pair of sleeps I found myself in the
kitchen with Glory, filling a picnic basket.

"A shady grove near a stream, a stone bench," I said.

"Right you are," she replied.

"Without throwing the Switch?"

"Again, yes," she answered, adding napkins and a
matching tablecloth. "Ready now."

I raised the basket.

"Lead on," I said.

I followed as she turned away and walked down the small hallway off the kitchen's rear.

"I don't recall there being an arboretum up this way," I said, thinking back to the post-Urtch search.

She laughed softly and halted before an unfamiliar door. When she opened the door and entered, it proved to be the entrance to a small area holding a few odds and ends of equipment. Closing the door behind us, she turned and took a step. Immediately, the room vanished, to be replaced by a rolling green field dotted with wildflowers, leading off toward a distant hilly area. Ahead and to the left, a line of trees bordered what must be a stream. Birds passed among them, and after a brief walk I heard a faint gurgling sound.

"Virtual reality setup," I said. "Nice trick."

"We can set reality levels here," she said, "even making things more real than your own reality, should we wish. I usually just call it the multi-purpose room."

"More real than real. Now that might be worth experiencing," I said, as I helped her unpack the basket and spread our fare. "How real is it right now?"

"If you were to fall into the stream you could drown in it," she replied.

"What do you use it for, besides picnics?"

"It's multi-purpose," she said.

"You already told me that. Show me what it can do."

"All right."

She looked past me, out from the grove, across the field toward the hills. Abruptly, the countryside vanished.

We stood in a gray place of diffuse lighting, three-dimensional clusters of variously-colored tubes extending in most directions. Globes of yellow light drifted within the tubes, taking turns at their junctions.

"It looks like a big schematic," I said, "only at an enormous level of complexity. The insides of a microprocessor, perhaps."

"These, I believe, might have been distant ancestors."

With her fingertip, she traced a small rectangle in the air before her. It assumed a bright, metallic opacity, covered with numbers or letters in a language I could not read. She touched a small red spot at its lower right-hand corner then, and the characters changed each time her finger moved. As they did, the area about us flowed from one prospect to another. Finally, she simply held it depressed and the characters flowed. So did our surroundings. I clenched my teeth and fists and waited. At length, she slowed it, then stopped it. I beheld another set of schematics.

"There," she said. "Name a primary or secondary color."

"Green," I said.

"All right," she told me. "That shall be the color of its walls and spires."

"What's walls and spires?"

"This city," she replied.

Then her hands began to move, darting forward, passing somehow into the tubes, pushing glowing balls through junctions, creating new tubes and junctions as if she were shaping dough. She directed some of the spheres down these new courses.

"What are they?" I asked. "The glowing balls?"

"What you would call electrons," she replied, extracting one and tossing it to me. I caught it. It was near-weightless, neither hot nor cold, and yielded to pressure like a tennis ball.

I tossed it back.

"What are you making?"

"The shaping of a seed," she replied. "I chose this one because I've worked with the model before and recalled some easy ways to make minor changes."

I shook my head.

"Is it all simulation?" I said. "Or were you doing something real?"

"Both," she said. "Either. You'll see. We can use it however we would. This is a design and manufacturing center, among other things. Multi-purpose."

"And you just edited an existing design?"

"Yes."

"To what?"

"Those things you spoke of . . . ?"

"Microprocessors?"

"Yes. Think of a complex of billions of them, each serving special ends. Think of them as having access to tiny manipulators which can be ordered to create more of themselves. Think of a master program which switches them on and off in various appropriate sequences. Now imagine them as having access to the necessary raw materials to fulfill their programs."

I laughed.

"It sounds like a genetic code. But since you said 'city' it must be an inorganic artifact."

She raised her hand and traced the rectangle again. This time she pressed a sequence of colored places along its top. Immediately she had finished, the structure collapsed in upon itself, imploding to a bright point, leaving us to regard it there in the gray place of diffuse lighting.

"Yes," she said, and she stooped and picked up the

golden mote. Rising, she touched my right fist, which I had not noticed was still clenched. "Open," she said.

I did so, and she deposited a tiny seed on the palm of my hand.

"Don't lose it," she said. So I closed my hand and held it. Then, taking my arm, "This way."

We took only a few paces along a rocky trail which had suddenly appeared beneath our feet, blue sky overhead, bright sun behind. Looking back and downward, I beheld a greener plain, perhaps a half-mile distant, running up to a line of trees.

"Is that our picnic area way over there?" I asked.

"Yes."

"I hope the virtual ants didn't get at the sandwiches. If they can be as real to them as the tablecloth is to the table—"

"Pick a spot," she said.

"Is that a proposition?"

"No. I want you to cast your seed upon the ground."

"There's a biblical injunction against that sort of thing."

"Plant that designer seed anywhere you wish—or just toss it onto a likely spot around here."

"Okay."

I knelt, brushed back a little dirt, laid the seed on that spot, brushed some over it.

"Now what?" I asked.

"That's it. You're finished."

I rose.

"What now?"

"We walk back and have our lunch."

She took my hand and we walked the walk.

· · ·

From our picnic area, we did have a view of the rocky hill where I'd planted the thing. Nothing untoward occurred during the next half-hour or so, though, and I almost forgot about it.

"Shall I uncork the wine now?"

"Please."

Then, almost between eyeblinks, the surface of the distant hill was altered, losing its gentle curves.

"Damn!" I said.

"Here. Let me." She reached for the bottle.

"No. It's that hilltop." I gestured.

"Ah. Yes, it's starting."

An irregular line worked its way across the hill, continuing a constant stirring along its length. It pushed itself higher, also.

I finally opened the bottle, poured us two glasses.

The city's pace of development seemed to increase as we watched. Slow at first, it rose higher, beating out the rate at which the hilltop sank. Soon its towers grew visibly, almost swaying, as its walls broadened and rose.

"Now this has to be a virtual readout of the seed's program, right?" I asked.

She sipped her wine.

"It is whatever I want it to be, dear Alf, whatever I choose to make it. This is omniality, remember? I could even reverse it and make the city go to seed."

"Most cities do that on their own, anyway. Says more about citizens, though, than it does about cities."

The sunlight glinted on the spires, which had taken on a distinctly greenish coloration.

"One can set up a world for habitation in a day's time, this way," she said.

"I'll bet you have other seeds you might sow that could overwhelm the other guy's," I said.

"Yes, and there are counters to those, and counters to those," she said. "It's a memorable sight to see an entire planetary surface awash in colors—overwhelming each other, falling back, rising to the top."

"How might something like that end?"

"I once saw a totally furnished world. Every possible spot was taken. But no one could live there. Too much had been planted by the warring factions. The planet's resources were exhausted."

"A whole world—wasted."

"Well, no. The matter was settled elsewhere—whether by war or money, I forget—and the winner came back and seeded a total breakdown for a return to basics, then started over again on a smaller scale. Place needed a lot of landscaping later, though."

I took another drink and watched the spreading city.

"Could we have taken that seed and planted it somewhere on the surface of the Earth and still produced the city?"

"Yes."

"But here in omniality we can just shut it down and file it away when the picnic's over?"

"Yes."

"Your technology fascinates me," I said. "It's a wonder we can talk to each other at all."

"I've had the advantage of living through your history."

"True. And you know where we're headed."

"Only in general ways. And it's not immutable, as I tried to tell you earlier."

"You're not really going to ride this thing all the way back to your own times, are you?"

"We've ridden it this far."

"You said yourself that the Earth doesn't even go that distance."

"Well, there's that. But we've still a goodly way to go."

"You're looking for something, aren't you? Hunting after some event in time you're not certain about—or some turning point. It's a probability thing, isn't it?"

"Which question do you want me to answer first? Yes, there is an element of probability there, as in everything. Who knows what we might find? And the nature of the beast determines its disposition."

I refilled our glasses.

"Still not giving anything away, are you, Medusa?"

Her hand moved nearer mine, our fingers intertwined. We watched the emerald city rise before us.

FIVE · BRAINS AND BISCUITS

Finally, the emerald city slowed in its growth and came to a halt. I applauded lightly.

"Well-citied, lady."

She clinked her glass against my own and we finished the wine.

Then she rose and nodded toward her handiwork.

"The tour, of course," she said.

"Of course," I responded, and we linked arms and hiked off toward the city singing, "We're off to see the wizard."

"You say that you really are a writer for an American magazine," she said, after catching her breath.

"I not only say it, I am."

"Does that mean you'll be going home once you've gathered enough material?"

"Be serious," I said. "I don't have a story. No one's going to believe all this. I just want to be here with you."

"I like your attitude, Alf," she said, and she entered the gates of the city and took me in.

We wandered the streets and galleries, then took high bridges over broad thoroughfares, had views from a dozen lofty apartments. Moving like green thoughts in a green brain, we explored tunnels, parks, plazas, commercial districts. The place was quiet save for our voices, our footfalls, our echoes, and a few creaks of settling structures.

It was as I swung my left foot forward, passing beneath an archway, that I knew it would come from my right— whatever *it* was. And Glory was to my left.

I felt my body relaxing downward into my midsection as, with the motion of my left foot, I kept all of my weight on the right and pivoted on it, drawing the left back, inward.

Suddenly, two men came around the corner at my right. The nearer threw a punch at me. The one to his right was reaching for Glory. Then another came into view behind them. I struck immediately, with my left foot, at the nearest shin. I felt a satisfying grating as the man's expression turned to one of pain. With the second knuckle of the second finger of my left hand, I drove a blow into the hollow of his right temple, most of my weight behind it. He began to fall, but I caught hold of him, turned him slightly, and pushed him into the man who was reaching for Glory.

Continuing my turning motion to my left, letting my arms lead it, I dropped to my left knee, raising my right fist to somewhere in the vicinity of my left ear. I uncoiled immediately as I rose, driving my right elbow into the low midsection of the second man.

Then I was rising as he was bending forward—in slow motion, it seemed—and my left hand rose and fell, striking him across the back of his neck, my weight sinking again with the strike.

Pivoting leftward as he fell, to where the man I had knocked off-balance with the body of the first had recovered, I leapt over his fallen companion. The man snapped a kick and threw a punch at me. I slid my left foot forward, turning, avoiding the kick, parrying the punch. My left arm passed behind him as I continued the turn, hand falling to rest upon his left shoulder.

I attacked his eyes with my right hand, but he was able to catch my wrist. Immediately, I raised my left hand from his shoulder, caught hold of his left ear, and, with a twisting, wrenching movement, tore it loose.

He screamed and his grip on my right wrist wavered as I let my left hand fall back to his shoulder, dropped my center, turned and, continuing my attack on his eyes, took him over backwards. As he struck the ground, my right elbow dropped to strike him in the solar plexus. This brought him partway upright again, and a perfect target for the blow that crushed his larynx.

I rose, still alert, but there were no others. I brushed dust from my left knee. Glory spat once, to her left, and I glanced at her in time to see her tongue dart, her lower jaw change position.

"Getting rid of some venom?" I asked.

She shrugged, then smiled. "Reflex," she said. "You're a very good fighter, Alf."

"Grew up in a tough neighborhood," I said.

"That was not tough neighborhood fighting, Alf. Those were killing techniques. You know them well and you used them without hesitation. The seven clones all had reputations as deadly warriors. Even Pietro, the artist, was a brawler—hung out with Cellini a good deal."

I gestured.

"So who might these guys be, and why do you think they attacked us?" I asked.

Even as I spoke, they vanished like pictures from a screen.

"Nobody in particular," she replied. "Omniality's Central Casting sent them over when I UHFed my wishes on the way up here."

"Testing. You could have just asked me," I said. "I'd have told you I'm pretty good in a scrap. Even studied a little self-defense technique, here and there."

"That was all offense, Alf."

"Generic term," I said. "Thanks for showing me the city. Is there anything else?"

"Don't be angry," she said. "It was too good an opportunity to pass up. No real danger. Let me show you the rest of the place. There is a lovely apartment with a master bedroom in the highest spire. Wonderful view."

She took my arm.

"No more surprises?"

"Only pleasant ones," she said.

• • •

Nor was she incorrect. Later, we lay for a long while, drowsing, watching through the spire's great window as the day dimmed over our deserted city. An almost spiritual feeling of satisfaction came upon me in my sated state as I watched the spire's long, pointed shadow go forth, along with those of the domes at its base. I remarked, "Hsssss."

"'Hssss,'" she replied.

"Hs hsss."

"Hss. Thank you."

"You've installed a day-night cycle here."

"Yes, everything for verisimilitude," she said.

I stretched and sat up. "Shall we go and walk under the stars? Head back to our grove?"

"Hs— Damn!" she said. "Stars. I forgot. Sorry." She raised a hand and pointed at the sky. A bright point of light burst within the heavens. "There," she said. "A promise. It will hold us until I can fetch more."

She sat up and fumbled after her clothing. I did the same. The landscapes of our bodies were fiery in the red star's light.

Minutes later, arms about each other, we entered the lift and plunged earthward. As we passed out of the city she gestured lightly and a sprinkling of stars occurred in the eastern half of the sky. "They figure in the earliest consciousness of the race," she commented. "Some anthropologists tell us that the earliest myths, with their hopes, fears, and ideals, had their roots in the constellations. Or was it the other way around? No matter. Religion, philosophy, tales of adventure and romance may all go back to the pictures in the sky." She gestured again and the Big Dipper appeared.

"Uh, how does a dipper figure in religion, philosophy, and romance?" I asked.

She paused, there on the hilltop, and stared at it, wrinkling her nose in a most becoming fashion. "You want to talk principles or you want to talk cases?" she asked.

"Sorry."

"You want religion and philosophy—romance and adventure, too—there!" She waggled a finger at the western sky and a constellation I had never seen before appeared—a great snaky showpiece twisted into the rough approximation of a figure eight, glowing with a multicolored mass of gemlike stars.

"My God! That's lovely!" I said.

"From my home world—Serpena—Ouroboros can be seen. And there is God's Web, from Arachne V." She indicated its net-like lineaments in the northeast. ". . . And the Reflected Face," she said, pushing aside the Dipper to hang a blazing countenance, only vaguely human, at midheaven.

Walking on, discussing life, cosmology, ethics, and the fine structure constant, she continued to rearrange the skies, announcing, periodically, "The Finger of Manu," "Mother Tree," and "Heaven's Staff Car."

Finally, with great care and explanation, she created some of her own, to demonstrate the complexes of psychological, anthropological, and animistic/philosophical notions which must have colored our primitive ancestors' thinking when they turned their gaze skyward. Glory's own constellations were graceful, profound, to the point.

Gathering our picnic supplies, we moved to exit the world she had made, somehow wiser, pleased that our relationship had graduated from the merely physical to higher intellectual levels where we experienced each other's thought processes with amazing congruity and full agreement as to life's major values and the ends of philosophy.

Reaching for the door to our other reality, I bade the night good night.

Back in our kitchen drinking a cup of coffee, I did a sudden review of my situation: If I were to believe what I had been told, I was a clone, identical to seven guys hanging in the Hellhole. I was also, somehow, from the distant future. For these reasons, Adam had made me a temporary junior executive so that he could keep an eye on me. Medusa, my Glory, may or may not have set out initially to seduce me only to learn what information she could, but now it was for real. Now it was genuine affection we felt for each other. Of course, she had learned everything she could about me along the way. . . .

I had to admit that I hadn't thought much lately concerning my ability to defend myself, as the need to do so had not occurred in recent years. Had I really picked all that up on the street, in the old neighborhood? I knew I hadn't gotten it at Brown.

"Glory," I said, looking across the room to where she was preparing herself a small ethnic dish I did not wish to scrutinize too closely, "I want to get to the bottom of this thing as badly as you do, so here's my plan."

"Yes?" she responded.

"I am going to finish my coffee, throw the Switch, and wish myself to my office at *Rigadoon* magazine in New York."

"They may be closed. Hard to say what the time will be."

I shrugged.

"In that case, I will go to my apartment and call my boss, Jerome Egan. It's no coincidence that I was given this

assignment—not with my clones hanging around in there."
I gestured toward the Hellhole. "I've got to find out how it
came about, who set it up. I've got to learn how I could be
the two different people I'd pretty much have to be."

"And if you can learn that?"

"I'll come back and tell you, and we can figure out what
to do about it."

"Either that, or it will remind you of your agenda, and
when you return we will no longer be friends."

"Granting that such a thing might happen, you have no
way of knowing it for certain."

She shook her head, a slow undulation.

"Then you shall accompany me, to learn for yourself
whatever I learn."

She tasted the thing in the pan and smiled, then transferred it to a dish.

"And if I learn something terrible shall I kill you?" she
asked.

I laughed, a little too tightly.

"We all do what we must," I said. "Sometimes that
includes trust."

She cut a portion of the fare and ate it. "Very well," she
said then. "I'll go with you."

We both laughed. I watched her sharp teeth flash as I
finished my coffee.

Looking eminently rested and respectable in the foyer's
small mirror, I moved to the niche and threw the Switch.
Then I went to the door and flung it wide. Evening shadows
lay upon the Etruscan Forum.

"Morning in New York," I said. "I think my timing's
good."

Then my gaze was caught by a wine bottle where before I had seen a bundle of rags. I stooped and retrieved it from the entranceway, held it up, and turned it slowly.

"Strange shape," Glory remarked.

I passed it to her.

"Classic Klein bottle format," I said, "the visualization of which was once explained by Isaac Asimov as follows: Imagine a goose that bends its neck forward and begins eating its way downward into its own midsection. After a time, its head emerges from its anus and it opens its beak wide. Quietus. Freeze-frame. This is how these things are done."

"Fascinating," she said, setting it atop a side-table as I secured the door. "And that is the bottle you gave to Urtch?"

"Yes. Ruffino."

She nodded and took my arm.

"The universe chooses to address us in a typical fashion. Take me to your office, Alf."

"Indeed, m'lady."

I adjusted my ascot, visualized, and wished.

A moment later we stood in my office in Manhattan. I cast a quick glance about me. Everything seemed to be where I'd left it.

"They don't seem to have fired me in my absence," I said.

I opened my door and stepped into the larger, outer office.

Empty. Still. According to the clock, it should be bustling. I moved to the nearest desk and consulted its day-calendar.

"Sunday," I announced. "It's what I get for losing track. Easily remedied, though. We can wish our way back, then have the singularity deliver us two days ago, or tomorrow. . . ."

"No!" she said. "It's not good to play with Time in matters which ultimately involve Time."

"A future superstition?"

"More than that. There are ways for Time to gang up on you."

"Okay. No problem. I'll just phone Jerry from here." I returned to my office, got an outside line, punched his number.

"Jerry," I said, "it's me, Alf."

"Where are you?"

"Here in town. At the office."

"Was there a story? Or are you writing it off?"

"No story yet, but there's a lot of interesting material. I just came back for a few things I need. I wanted to ask you something about this assignment, though."

There followed a silence. Then, "Like what?" he said.

"Oh, how it came to be—just now. Why I got—"

"Alf. Go home."

"But—"

"Just go home and wait."

He hung up.

"We're meeting at my apartment," I said. "Is it okay to jump back to Rome and then jump there, so long as I don't mess with Time? Or—"

"Take a taxi," she told me.

Growling, I led her through the offices. How could I have been plotting bizarre plots when I remembered working here for so long?

We descended and walked a couple of blocks before we located a cab. It was easy to be spoiled by the Hellhole.

My place was as I had left it, relatively neat—as the cleaning lady had been by that final morning—and I showed Glory the living room, dining room, kitchen, and den. We entered the bedroom, where she gazed at the king-sized bed, and said, "We really ought to, before we go back."

"Indeed," I replied. "It would be a shame—" and the callbox buzzed.

"Alf here," I said.

"There's a Mr. Egan wants to see you."

"Send him up," I said.

I felt a strong need to empty my bladder.

"Excuse me, Glory," I said. "Won't be but a minute."

After I'd switched on the light and closed the bathroom door behind me, however, I'd a feeling it might be a little more than a minute. It had to do with the way my reflection maintained eye contact while talking to me:

"Alf," it said, "don't try to make it a dialogue. Just listen. I am your earlier self, and this message is a post-hypnotic implant. It could only be set off if you were working on the soul-swapper story, had returned for information concerning the assignment, and had a message that your boss was on his way to see you. That triggered the bladder reflex and the present ambience is stimulus for the rest. You must remember that I am Paul Jensen—meaning that you were Paul Jensen. This will self-explain in a few minutes. I have ranged up and down several decades to set this up. The rest should self-explain later. Ask Jerry all the questions you were going to ask him. Then, afterwards, ask him to dowse your apartment. This is very important. We've concealed—"

There came a knocking on the door.

"Yes?" I asked.

"I believe your boss is just outside," she said.

"Wait a minute. Don't let him in," I told her. "First, go to the shorter chest of drawers, across the room from the foot of the bed. Third drawer down. Get me a fresh pair of shorts."

"Sure thing, Alf."

The post-hypnotic had not included any special relief for the micturition response. Hence, my bladder had decided to take care of itself while I listened to my earlier self, and I hadn't even noticed till Glory knocked. I'd have to remember that if I ever set up another of these. Too bad about the end of the message, though.

There came a short knock, the door opened a few inches, and a slim hand entered, bearing a pair of my shorts.

"Thanks."

After cleaning myself and tossing the damp ones into the hamper, I let myself out and followed the voices to the living room.

"Jerry," I said, "thanks for being so prompt. This is Glory. She works at—"

"Yes, we've met," he responded, wringing my hand more briskly than usual. He took a step toward a chair, paused, and said, "Terribly busy week. You have some problem with the current job?"

"No, no problem," I said. "Just something concerning how it came about. Sit down and let me get you a cup of coffee—or something stronger, if you'd like."

He made a show of looking at his watch.

"What the hell. Make it a Scotch and soda," he said.

"Glory?"

"A tough, dry, red wine."

"Okay."

"What's wrong with this picture?" I said. "I got the soul-changer assignment."

"It's your sort of story. You've always enjoyed investigating the oddball, off-the-beaten-track sort of thing."

"Agreed. But this time there was more to it—some directive, some pressure, some caution to secrecy."

He sighed and stared into his glass. Then he nodded and took a sip.

"Yes, there was a telephone call. From one of the publishing company's owners. He said he wanted the story covered now. And he wanted you to do it. I was not to mention his name."

"How about half of his name?" I asked. "Like if I were to say 'Paul'?"

"And I were to say 'Jensen'?"

"Yes," I replied. "Actually, it's fairly innocuous. We're related, and it looks like he thought he was doing me some sort of favor. It *is* my sort of thing, and he knew the place was not all that well-known. I think he wanted to give me an exclusive."

I took a drink.

"I'd rather you didn't mention I told you," he said.

"No, I won't. Nothing really turns on it now. I just wanted to check on a suspicion."

"I'll have to start being nicer to you."

I laughed. "One more thing," I said, "and you're ahead of the game."

"What's that?"

"I'd like you to dowse the apartment."

"Thinking of digging a well?"

"No, but I've misplaced something and I've heard that you guys can find anything."

"That's my old man. I'm rusty."

"Please."

"Sure. Get me a wire coathanger."

I went off to a closet and brought one back for him. He crimped it in the middle and bent both arms downward.

"All right," he said. "What are we looking for?"

"Give me a thrill and try without knowing," I said. "I've heard that it doesn't really matter."

He rose.

"So long as you don't do an article about it for someone else." Holding the hanger by its two arms he strolled the length of the room, entered the dining area, and turned left. "It's in the bedroom," he said, as he went in there.

We followed him. The hanger seemed to jerk to his right. Glory licked her lips and followed him toward the taller dresser, standing between the closet and bathroom doors. She followed him on his right, I on his left as he approached it. The wire jerked downward, indicating the second drawer. Glory reached forward and drew it open. Handkerchiefs and shorts to the right, rolled socks to the left . . .

. . . and I knew somehow, even before Jerry's hanger began drifting leftward. I reached forward, plunged my hand in among the socks, and felt around. Glory uttered a brief hiss as I located and withdrew a small, strangely heavy, cheap-looking, cloth-covered box. I flipped it open immediately to reveal a pair of oval, gray metal cuff links inscribed with a Celtic design.

"That what you were looking for, Alf?" Jerry asked.

"Yes. Thank you very much."

"Hardly anyone wears cuff links these days," he observed.

"I do have a use for them and these are of particular sentimental value," I said, suddenly somehow understanding exactly where the value lay, as I withdrew the links from the case and handed them to Glory. "Here. Would you keep these for me?" I said. "Till I need them?"

Her eyes met mine as her fist closed upon the jewelry, and she smiled. I shut the case and moved as if to replace it among the socks. I palmed it as I did so, and after I closed the drawer I slipped it into the side pocket of my jacket.

"Let's go finish our drinks," I said.

After Jerry left, Glory came across the room and into my arms.

"Thanks for the show of faith," she said. "You make it hard to doubt you."

I held her with my right arm, as I let my left hang to the side to cover the box in my pocket against her quick frisking movements. After all, I could have picked up something else in the bathroom.

"I told you that's how it would be," I said.

"What are their significance?" she asked.

"I have no idea. I've never seen them before. Didn't know they were there. You must have ways of testing objects for unusual properties."

She nodded. "Of course. And what of this Paul Jensen?"

"A great-uncle, well-heeled, somewhat eccentric. Always kindly disposed toward me. Haven't seen him in years, though. It may take a while to run him down and learn his interest in this."

"Then let's go test the links," she said.

Double-wish, and we were in the foyer, facing the living room where one sofa was totally dominated by a crustaceous-looking individual five or six feet in length who, in the claw at the end of one of its many articulated limbs, held a great mug of what looked to be swamp water. Membranous wings of indeterminate outline were draped over the cushions at its back, and its head was covered with a forest of short antennae. The head, which was apple-green, darkened on our appearance. A dull metal, tube-like canister stood upon the floor before it. The side facing me bore a grid, and what appeared to be a small control panel. Its uppermost end was covered by some clear material, and when I moved nearer later I detected within its shadowy recesses contours strongly suggesting those of a human brain.

Adam Maser Macavity, the Kaleideion, stood before it, left foot on an ottoman, left elbow on left knee, left hand supporting his chin. He had on a black suit and a white shirt opened at the neck, and he held a drink in his right hand. He was leaning forward listening to the buzzing noises the creature made. These sounds ceased immediately on its regarding us.

"Why, hello," Adam stated, smiling, and lowering his left hand. "Allow me to introduce Gomi, the most interesting messenger I've ever encountered." Then, "Gomi, these are my associates, Alf and Medusa. We're all in this together."

Gomi nodded his antennae. "It is good to meet the lady who makes men stiff," he said buzzingly, "and the man who is a sacred river."

Adam raised his eyebrows. "Sacred river?" he said.

"'In Xanadu did Kubla Khan a stately pleasure dome decree,'" Gomi buzzed, giving me a beat in which to come in and finish, "'Where Alf the sacred river ran through caverns measureless to man.'"

Adam groaned, while I grinned at Gomi. Glory just stared and said, "That is awful."

Gomi's buzzings followed the rhythms of laughter and he raised his brackish-looking drink, sipping off some of the small mushrooms that floated on its surface. Noting Glory's gaze, "Tastes worse," he said. "But you wouldn't want to be in the same room as an alien with *turista*."

"Thought you guys always did it on the wing," Adam said.

"If we're not careful," Gomi agreed.

"That's bad," Glory stated.

"Not as bad as upchucking in null-grav," Gomi responded, "especially if you've been eating pizza. Grab a seat. Grab anybody's seat."

Glory and I lowered ourselves to nearby cushions.

"Gomi and I met over a million years ago," Adam told us. "Gomi's a messenger, as I said—for off-planet intelligences."

"Freelance courier, actually," the creature corrected. "The message doesn't fly unless there's something in it for me."

"What constitutes the message?" Glory asked.

Gomi tapped the canister with one of his claws. "The medium, of course. I'm really good at paring things down to bare essentials."

Glory moved nearer and peered into the container.

"Oh," she said.

"Yes, I screw my brains out and then I've got it—intelligence in a tube. As in, 'What's in the can, man?'"

"What then?"

"In my case, it goes to the highest bidder. There're lots of XTs who'd love to explore and discover and meet interesting new people and interrogate them. Haven't the time or the resources to manage it personally, though. So they have standing orders with those of my sort. One may just have an interest in the arts, or philosophy, or the sciences, or theology. Another may only be into the evolution of sea creatures. Another may just want to follow the development of a particular concept among quadrupeds. Someone else may be into cold-blooded thought, or the brains of those living in binary systems. These wish-lists are all posted along the ways. We may consult them after coming across something interesting, or we may go shopping after we learn of someone's special needs."

"'Ways'?" Glory asked. "What ways?"

"Gomi's is one of the few natural space-faring races," Adam said. "They come equipped with the ability to negotiate the undersides of spacetime as we normally perceive it, making their ways from world to world entirely under their own power. They spread their wings like the sails on ancient sea vessels and let the symmetry pressures of the ways propel them."

"They may be the universe's stretch-marks," Gomi said, "or a demonstration that at certain levels space can be eroded, or the game trails of underside beasts whose spoor writes its own rules where they pass—for sometimes we encounter unusual roadkill and hear strange barks and lows across the parsecs. My people are not great theoreticians in this area, since we already have all we need of it."

"Clear sailing and a fair wind to Arcturus," Adam said.

"Yo ho ho," Gomi added.

"Life on the dancing waves."

"Brain waves."

"Yes, about that," Glory put in. "Why just the brains?"

"The parties interested in the development of intellect under various conditions are interested mainly in just that—intellect," Gomi replied.

"So you just leave the bodies and take them the brains?" I said.

"Well, I get the best deals I can for the bodies whenever there's an opportunity. But yes, mass is extremely important on trips of that sort, and my kind does seem to have a knack for ultra-highspeed neurosurgery."

It clicked its claws once and took another drink. "We've gotten it down to a real art. Pretty much have to, for getting ahead in the world."

"What's special about that one?" I asked, nodding toward the canister.

"It contains the first complete map of the human collective unconscious," Gomi replied. "Lucky find. Worth a great deal. I was going to run it off to old Yog, who has a strong interest in stuff like that, when I ran into Macavity here. He made me an offer I couldn't refuse. Do you know I've been to the depths, I've been to the heights, I've collected brains on worlds all over the place, and there's half a universe I'd never seen?"

"No," Adam said, "but if you'll hum a few bars I'll try to fake it."

Gomi immediately broke into a raucous, chirping laughter; then, letting up, issued a high, piercing humming that hurt my ears. I almost thought at that time that I also detected a fast UHF exchange between Glory and Adam, using it for cover.

Glory hissed a simple tune then and I tried "I've been to the depths" in my deepest voice. Adam issued a long series of screeches and yowls. A strange sound even emerged from the canister.

Finally, I said, "So what did he give you for the thing?"

"Can't you guess?" Gomi replied. "A sense of humor. I'm the only one of my kind ever to have one, and it's great—seeing the wacky side of life and the ironies. No more being mocked as 'one of those humorless flying clods' by the other races I encounter. I've got some zingers now will knock them over. In fact—I have this ambition of being a standup, fly-by-night comedian. Make the circuit of the worlds, do my shticks. A funny thing happened to me on my way through subspace. Ran into one of my relatives and our parcels got switched while we were talking. Hope his customer likes hot fungi sandwiches from the old country. His canister had a rare twenty-second-century synthoid bookkeeping brain, a thing I didn't even realize till a lot later. Maybe the hot mustard masked it. There's just no accounting for it. C'mon! Give me a break! You an audience or an oil painting? Maybe you'd like I should do some *pro bono* brain switching? Hey, professor, let's have a little hard claw music!"

It rose, humming, and executed an eight-legged tap-dance about the foyer. I applauded lightly, hoping the creature would stop soon, as some of the more delicate pieces of furniture looked threatened. The others joined my clapping. Gomi took this as a call for an encore, however, and accompanying himself with an even higher-pitched humming, did a faster number about the room, disagreeing only with an end-table and a rocker.

"Fine stage presence and timing," Adam said, "considering he only got his sense of humor a few minutes before you came in."

"Indeed," I said.

"Of course," Glory added.

At that, Gomi bowed and was seated again. ". . . And a replacement brain of perhaps equal value," it said. "You work out those coordinates yet, Macavity?"

Adam passed over a piece of paper covered with notations. "Yes. Can you read them all right?"

Half of the antennae flicked toward the paper. "Clear enough. Clear enough. I get there, *exactamente*, for a very special brain. Thanks. Hope you enjoy yours."

It finished its drink, rose to its numerous appendages, unfurled its wings, and was gone, leaving behind the canister it had brought.

"'Not snow, no, nor rain, nor heat, nor night keeps them from accomplishing their appointed rounds,'" said Adam, rising to his feet and saluting. Then he stretched.

"No, but I'm sure this one breaks for graffiti, breaks for heads and breaks them—and when it learns that it'll get a laugh in certain quarters it'll doubtless learn to break wind."

"You had that one ready," he said, "which means that you anticipated mine. That's scary."

"I don't admit to anything," I said, "but I wouldn't mind catching that act once he's got it polished."

Glory gave me a strange look and refrained from hissing.

"And speaking of polish," I continued, remembering the cuff links, "we've picked up a little something . . ."

But before I could finish, the front door burst open and a familiar voice yelled, "And she was going to shoot me too. Then I was here, thank God!"

That's what I got for not being quick enough to flick the Switch.

• • •

She was Morgan Barry, actress, and I'd been a fan ever since I'd done a full takeout on her when I was writing features for *OnStage* magazine. She came tearing into the reception room like a blond Valkyrie shouting, "Which one is the goddamn soul-changer?"

I'd spent three weeks with her, putting the story of her strange career together. She was sweet, warm, appealing to the public, cooperative and hardworking with her colleagues. She had everything going for her except the one kink that was crippling her progress. She was a jinx.

Mama Baumberg was devoted to romantic literature and had named her Morgan after Morgan le Fay, the fairy sister of King Arthur, because she wanted her daughter to enchant and captivate the whole world. Better Mama should have named her after Mordred, the bad-news knight who ruined the Round Table.

So Morgan Baumberg became Morgan Barry, actress, and wherever she went back luck was sure to follow: props failed, sets collapsed, lights exploded, cameras jammed. The entertainment business is particularly vulnerable to superstitions—never whistle in a dressing room, never throw a hat on a bed, never wish a performer good luck—so of course everybody was afraid to work with this charming hoodoo.

Not so charming now. She glared at me. "You!"

"Yes. May I introduce Adam Maser, the goddamn soul-changer?"

"My God, you're red!"

"And his assistant, Glory."

"This is Morgan Barry, a magnificent actress, also known as Voodoo Barry."

"Did you have to print that, damn you? Is that why you stopped seeing me?"

"Morgie, I still love you, but the piece was finished."

She described me with a four-letter word, then turned the Valkyrie on Adam. "I want my luck changed." But there was no resisting his warm smile and she returned it. "Please, kind sir?"

"Now what's all this brouhaha, Ms. Barry? You're obviously dressed for dinner . . . beautifully. Where? What happened? Why'd you wish here?"

"Cafe En Coeur, just across from the UN. I was there with Mal Mawson, one of my producers, and a potential backer. Mal brought me along to help coax the guy into putting up front money for a new series, 'Country Western,' about two Nashville singers who solve mysteries."

I said, "Oy."

"I'm going to be Wendy Western, who sings—no dubbing—and does all the shooting with a six-gun," the Valkyrie informed me. "Any compliments beyond 'Oy'?"

"And this is the shooting you were shouting about when you entered, Ms. Barry?" Adam asked.

"No. We were having drinks before dinner, laughing it up, softening him up, when damn if the backer's wife didn't appear out of nowhere and shoot him, and I got the hell out of there to here."

"Why?" I asked.

"Why?! I was probably next."

"I mean why'd she shoot him and maybe you?"

"From what she was screeching, she thought we were having an affair."

Adam and Glory had their eyes fixed on Morgan as though they were looking right through her. There was a long silence. At last Morgan snapped, "Well?"

"Wait," I said.

"For what?"

"They're talking."

"Talking! They aren't even moving their—"

"They're talking UHF. Ultra High Frequency."

"Not to me, they aren't. They—"

Adam broke in. "Sorry, Ms. Barry. We *have* been talking. UHF, as Alf said, but not to you. We've been talking to your brother."

"Brother? What brother? I haven't got any brother."

"This will come as a shock to you, but you do have a brother and he's here."

"Here? Where? There's only the four of us."

"Inside you."

"What? Brother? Inside? Me?" Morgan shook her head incredulously. "You're crazy."

"Please sit down and listen. Yours is a fascinating problem which my assistant has already solved. There will be no more bad luck."

Morgan sank down, dumbfounded. I wasn't exactly on top of it myself.

"Do be patient," Adam continued. "When your mother conceived, fraternal twins developed, brother and sister. But during the gestation, the sister embryo overgrew the brother embryo, engulfed him and incorporated him in yourself as a fraternal cyst. This is unusual but not unique. There have been many such cases."

"I . . . I did a dreadful thing like that?" Morgan stammered.

"Not consciously. Not deliberately," Glory assured her. "How could you? It was pure accident."

"I f-feel like a cannibal."

"Nonsense," Adam laughed. "Your brother's alive, and *that's* unique. He's an enclosed, living cyst, and he's lonely and irascible because he's isolated: no friends, no one to talk to."

"Wh-why has he never talked to me?"

"He can receive full frequency but can only transmit UHF, which infuriates him. And what's been worse for you, he's a warlock, a witch-cyst."

Adam paused long enough to allow it to sink in.

"Your brother's been your jinx. The most trivial things can sting him into casting malevolent spells. Your guest's cocktail conversation annoyed him so he put a stop to it via the jealous wife. He conjured that false conviction into her mind."

"How has Glory solved the problem?" I asked.

"She's promised him a friend. He won't be lonely and angry any more."

"Someone that hears and speaks UHF?"

"And your speech, too. A charming lady friend. It all depends on Ms. Barry."

"Wh-what depends on m-me?"

Macavity became his most beguiling, which was as overwhelming as his persona power. Or maybe it was the same thing. "How would you like to headline yourself with an unusual pet to be with you at all times: bright, friendly, captivating, an attention-getter?"

"Like Cheetah, Tarzan's chimp?" But I was ignored.

Morgan could only look at Adam with wide eyes. "I— I haven't the foggiest what you're talking about," she faltered.

"Bok Pang, one of the Panda crowd," Glory said. "Dammy's bringing her over for your brother—should arrive in a few days—and he swears that from now on he'll magic nothing but good luck for you."

"Go back to the Cafe En Coeur," Adam said. "The guest's alive. Your brother made his wife a lousy shot; didn't want you killed, too. The backer's so delighted to be the center of attention that he's putting up the front money."

Morgan shook her head. "It's all taken care of? The bad luck?"

"All. Wendy Western and Panda Bok are going to win Emmy awards."

"I can't believe it."

"Your brother's promise. Wish back and find out."

"I— What do I have to pay? I—"

"Forget it, Morgie," I broke in. "That piece I did on you for *OnStage* got me a fat contract with *Rigadoon*. I owe you. I'll take care of it."

She burst into tears, tried to kiss us all at the same time, and headed for the front door supported by Glory.

"I don't have to wish you luck," Adam said. "You've got it already."

Once we heard the door shut, Adam's hand moved past me to pick up the Klein Ruffino bottle.

"This thing, Alf," he said. "What's the scoop?"

"I gave a full bottle to an old bum named Urtch who'd turned up in an entranceway after the Switch was thrown."

"'Urtch'? As in 'Demiurtch'?"

"He just said 'Urtch.'"

Adam growled softly.

"And he did this to the bottle afterwards?"

"I didn't see him do it, but that's how I found it later."

"And he stayed out there while the Switch was on?"

"Insisted."

"What became of him?"

"He just sort of disappeared before I looked again."

"He do or say anything else interesting?"

"Tossed his first empty into the fog to show me a photon smear. When I told him I thought I saw something moving out there he said it was the Ouroboros Serpent."

"Hm. That tells me something about timing."

"Of what?"

"Oh, it's just a private superstition I— Gods! I've got it myself! The fresh superstition! I have an ingredient to donate! Excuse me." He picked up the brain canister and ran off toward the Hellhole. "Every little bit helps," he said.

I went to the kitchen and made hot chocolate. Later, while we were drinking it, Adam emerged, wiping his hands on his trousers, and threw himself down upon a sofa.

I poured a cup and took it to him.

"Challenging chocolate," he said tasting it. "The new ingredients add amazing dimensions."

"Are we drinking the same chocolate?" I asked, raising mine to sip again.

"Iddroid ingredients, Blackie. Just ran three simulations with what we've got and had a different result each time. It's definitely nonlinear now. The uncertainty of life will be in it. The inconnu!"

Glory came up on his other side and You-Hiffed at him. He held out his hand. She deposited my cuff links in it. He scrutinized them, weighing them with his hand.

He reached up, unzipped the air in front of him, reached inside the slit and drew forward a unit about the size of a can opener. It hung suspended before him.

"Parlor work station," Glory explained.

He attached a pair of wires from the unit and pressed a design on its front. Then he raised his eyes to read something it displayed.

"Beta Cygnus," he announced. "Earth design, metallic compound from Beta Cygnus," and he detached the leads, pushed everything back out of sight, and zipped space shut once more. Again, he bounced the links in his hand. Then, "Otherwise innocuous," he added. "No concealed transmitter, no hidden explosive. *Nada.*"

He handed them to me.

"You knew something was hidden in your apartment, but you did not know what," he said.

"That's right."

"Nan tells me you're aware of your identity with the clones."

"Correct."

"Then it would seem the cuff links are more in the nature of a reminder to you or a caution to me that something is in the offing—rather than any threat in themselves. Did their discovery set off any special chain of reminiscences or compulsions?"

"No," I said, truthfully, thinking of myself in the mirror—and happy that that was before the links discovery.

"Then I suggest you be alert for such at any time, and let me know if they do occur."

"All right." Whenever . . .

"Dammy, you still owe Alf, you know," Glory said. After all that had happened, I was surprised—and pleased—she still thought Macavity should keep his promises.

"I know. But I've already offered him a partnership."

"I mean the recall."

"The total? Of course! Idiot, I am. In time all will be made copacetic. Copacetic? Yes?"

"Not after 1940."

"Thanks again. I've decided against the total recall of that one-man band. Too limited in capacity. It'll be Marcel Proust instead."

"You've got him?"

"I've got the whole Green Carnation, *Yellow Book*, fin de siècle crowd. They used to come to me, pawning, buying exchanging for new kicks."

But Adam was interrupted by yet another invasion, a sort of Lord Byron, the poet, who declaimed, "The ITs shall inherit the earth!"

I stared. He was a tall, almost pretty-looking fellow who wore a navy blue cloak over gray trousers and jacket, a heavily ruffled shirt, and a red waistcoat. He had on black gaitered boots, and his hair was long and wavy. His eyes were pale, his smile bright, his voice amazing.

Macavity bowed lightly and observed, "Which would have you leading the way, Mr. Ash. Alf, I'd like to introduce Ashton Ash, lead vocalist for the IT, the most popular singing group of a generation."

Since it was not a generation with which I was familiar I could only smile, nod, and acknowledge, "Of course. The IT. Happy to know you, Mr. Ash."

"I find it hard to guess what you might possibly want," Macavity stated, slipping into the persona mode, tuned to make him seem larger, more forceful, spreading his presence throughout the room, dominating. "You're rich, talented, attractive—"

Ash eyed me and Glory almost wistfully. Finally, licking his lips, "Sex," he responded.

Macavity chuckled. "Some exotic enhancement?" he asked.

"No. Just the plain old-fashioned kind."

"Surely you're joking. You must have it thrust upon you constantly. I don't understand—"

"Of course. But I can't take advantage of it."

"Ah! Impotence. You don't need my services. There are many forms of medical treatment available."

Ash shook his head. Then he stood straighter, opened his mouth, and began to sing. It was Astrafeeamonte's wild, amazing aria from *The Magic Flute*. We listened, spellbound, to the entire thing. When he was finished we applauded.

"Amazing coloratura," Macavity said, just as Ash shifted to baritone for a barbershop number.

Afterwards, we simply stared. It was too much, that voice, with its extraordinary range, fluency, and shades of feeling. I'd never heard another like it.

"I don't understand," Macavity said. "Surely, you don't wish to trade a voice like that."

Ash looked at each of us in turn. Then, "We are all adults here," he announced, and he fumbled at his trousers and braces and dropped his pants.

I watched, fascinated, as did the others. He seemed well-enough hung to have no complaints, and I did not really understand the display until he seated himself, legs open.

"Aha!" Macavity said. "You're a true hermaphrodite! Remarkable! Do you know how rare that is?"

Ash smiled.

"It's rather common in the company I keep," he replied. "All of the IT are true hermaphrodites. It's the accompanying hormone mix that gives us our unique vocal abilities."

"Of course," Macavity said. "You are doubly—nay, triply—blessed."

"Cursed, rather," Ash responded.

"How so?"

"The few times I revealed all of my equipment I frightened away potential partners. It made me self-conscious, neurotic about the whole business. In fact, I've never really gotten any in my whole life—"

"*Sacré bleu!*"

"*Götterdamerung!*"

"*Pobrecito!*"

He nodded sadly.

"—which is why I'm here," he finished. And I heard Macavity mutter, "An *inconnu absolu!* Ingredient!"

Then, "Tell me your desire—besides the simple and basic—and you will be accommodated," he said.

"I want to trade one set of them—either one, I guess—so I can be like everyone else. Well, half of everyone else, anyway."

"You realize what it will do to your voice?"

"Yes, but I don't care. I've made my bundle, I'm ready to retire and enjoy life. Give some new IT a chance."

"All right. But I must have the entire ensemble. I'll provide you with a new set of solo equipment—of your choice—out of stock. Of equal or superior quality, I hasten to add."

Ash beamed.

"It's a deal." He rose, adjusted his apparel, and, with a nod to Glory and me, allowed the cat-man to lead him off into the Hellhole.

It wasn't long before Adam appeared.

"The job's done," he said, "but he'll need to sleep it off."

He paused a moment and glanced at Glory, who turned and headed for the kitchen.

"Now then," he continued. "I've been picking up Cagliostro's ingredients left and right, and there are just a few more tricky ones to go after. How's about you and Nan checking out another one for me?"

"Sure," I said. "Who, what, when, where, why, and how?"

"I already filled Nan in in the ultrahigh way; basically, I want you to jump back to the sixteenth century and see whether a sweet little old lady is indeed a specialized precog, as my research indicates she might be. If she is, see if there's anything she'd trade for it."

"Check," I said, "and a question."

"What?"

"I've been wondering why you were so taken by Cagliostro's scheme in the first place."

"Because it's there," he said. "All along, I knew that would turn up at what would prove to be a key moment. Your showing up at about the same time did a lot to reinforce the feeling."

I shrugged.

"And if I'm not whatever you think and if the Iddroid project fails . . . ?"

He grinned. "Then one day something else of equal interest will come along, and I will follow. Wherever my heart leads me, baby, I must go."

Glory came up, a small plastic sack in one hand. She asked him if he wanted a refill on the chocolate. "No," he said, "I've got to go now."

She shook her head. "I'm pulling rank," she told him. "*We* go now. You throw the Switch. While Ash is gone, take a nap. You're going to need the rest."

"Must I?"

"Yes. I want you in top shape, whatever happens."

He made a face. Then, "All right. I don't need it. But just for you," he said. He yawned, stretched with leonine grace, and rose to his feet. He followed us across the foyer to the niche.

As we wished out, he was reaching for the Switch. A moment later, Glory, sack in one hand, and I found ourselves on a muddy trail, a few bedraggled-looking trees about us, rain falling steadily.

"Bad timing," I growled.

She caught hold of my arm. "Can't call them all. That little cottage up ahead should be the place, though," she said. "Come on. By the way, we're in Knaresborough, in Yorkshire, and the year is 1521."

"And who's the woman?"

"Mother Shipton," she said. "Not too much is known about her, but—"

"Mother Shipton," I said, "the British prophetess—sure. She's supposed to have predicted the Great Fire of 1666 and a bunch of other events. The only catch is that like most such stuff these things are really impossible to document."

"Well, let's hope we can find out."

I studied the cottage. All of its shutters were secured, and a ribbon of smoke came up out of the chimney. Glory went directly to the front door and pounded on it.

"Hello?" she called. "Hello? Would you let two travelers in out of the rain?"

"Why the bloody hell should I?" came a woman's voice from within.

"Because it's the decent thing to do," I suggested. "But mainly, if you've had a vision of an important visit this time of year, this is it."

There came a rattling sound from the other side of the door, and moments later it was flung open. We stumbled inside and Glory pushed the door shut behind us as a squat, straggly-haired woman of middle height uttered a roar and sprang toward me. Her left hand struck at my face and her right made a grab for my groin. I retreated, parrying and blocking, so that my back came up against the door. She tried again and this time I caught her wrists and pushed her out to arms' distance and held her there.

"Will you accept an apology?" I asked. "Or should we just go?"

Her face took on a blank expression and her lips trembled. "Deliver us, O Lord, from the peril of the sword," she recited, "and the boxed ones from the power of the cat." Then she shook her head, backed up, and smiled. "Won't you have yourselves a seat?" she said, glancing upward to where water dripped from the rafters. "If you can find a dry one."

"'Scrying by aggression,'" Glory said, drawing up a bench that would hold both of us and positioning it between puddles. "That's why she never made the really big time."

"And you had to test it out on me."

"Of course. I already knew you could defend yourself." Glory passed the bag she'd brought to the woman who stood before us. Mother Shipton was wrapped in countless layers of nondescript dark garments. "I've brought some tea and biscuits," Glory said. "If you'd set some water to boiling we can have a hot drink and a bite to eat."

"Tea?" the woman said. "Excuse me, m'lady. I did not know—but no. You came with him out of the places I see darkly. It is all very confusing."

She turned away, filled a kettle from a pitcher, and hung it above the flames.

"Damned dry future of yours," she said. "I can see it so comfortable. *Your* roof doesn't leak."

"No," Glory said. "You're right." She reached into her jacket pocket and withdrew a silver flask. "Nip of brandy?" she suggested, unscrewing the cap, extending the container. "To warm us while we wait for the tea?"

The woman's eyes shone as she accepted and tossed back a healthy slug. "What brings you here?" she asked, wiping her mouth on the back of her hand and returning the flask.

"Wait," I said. "Before you two talk business I want to know the meaning of that bit of verse, right after you went for me."

She shook her head. "If they rhymes I don't always follow 'em," she said. "But I see you in the sky a hunter."

"What does that mean?"

"You must think the piece over carefully."

"How did you ever discover you possessed such an odd ability?" I asked.

"My husband was a schoolmaster," she said. "A decent man much of the week, he taught me my letters and numbers and many Latin tags. Come Saturday, though, he'd stop at the public house. Got the devil in him when he drank. Comin' home then, if he avoided trouble with his fellows, he would beat me. After a time, I noticed that he almost always came at me the same way. So the next time he did it I was ready. I stepped up close and gave him five good ones below the belt and a pair on the head. He was ready to stop then, right where he fell, and I was filled with visions of things to come. Some of them were his and mine, others showing wars, shipwrecks, fires. I wrote them all down. The next week I swung at him before he swung at me, and I got more. Soon I took to waylaying him on the way home, both to keep from messin' the place we lived in and because it often gave me a second chance at him later. See, I'd started writin' these pamphlets of predictions and they did pretty well. Made enough to buy this place, which was quite a step up in the world."

I looked around at the single room, with its counter, fireplace, well-worn bed, its few sticks of furniture, its leaks. I nodded.

"Oh, I could see ahead to how much better people will have it another day," she went on. "But at least I could aim for improvement. I took at last to waitin' outside the pub of a Saturday night and followin' certain departin' drinkers a ways—later givin' rise to stories of a temperance ghost. I beat on any of the ones who'd too much to drink, as they wouldn't remember well come next mornin'. I saw more and more that way, put out my pamphlets more regular, was able to fix this place up over what it was to begin with—like gettin' a floor."

"What about your husband?" I asked.

"Oh, he was none too happy with his aches and bruises," she said, "but at first he liked what I was doin' for our purse and the house. It sort of evened out."

"In my day, they call you Mother Shipton."

She nodded.

"Two sets of twins," she said. "When I was fourteen and again at sixteen. The girls married well. My Rob is a farrier, and my Jamie a cabinetmaker. They both have them good wives. Makes one mighty dry, talkin' like this."

Glory passed her the flask and she took a long swig.

"I don't see anything like a man's gear or clothing around here," I said.

She nodded. "My Dickon up and run off one Saturday night. Guess he just didn't have the stomach for more propheseyin'. They found him floatin' in the river next day. I'd seen it comin' but he never paid my warnings no heed. Could've married lots of times after that. As I said, I was gettin' on well-off. But I'd bring my suitors home and pound on 'em a bit. The first few larrups always tells me somethin' about the person, the others bring other visions."

"As when you said what you said about the sword and the cat?"

"Yes. Knew you for a hunter right away. Lots of danger."

"Such as?"

"That's the trouble with prophecies. You never get it all." She glanced at the kettle, which was just beginning to make noises. "I could see none of my swains would ever amount to much, so they never got much farther than being beaten. There was one or two as actually took a likin' to it, though, and they started comin' around for more . . . long as I was a little more careful." She smiled. "We actually had a couple of good things goin' for some time till they got too laid up. Men are strange."

"Because they are of the same race as women," I said.

She stared at me. Then she slapped my knee and laughed.

"You know whereof you speak, hunter," she said, accepting a biscuit from the box Glory had opened. "Mm! These are good!"

I got up and made the tea while she ate several more. I reached over and snagged one myself. In an odd way, it was almost cheery, being in a cold, leaky cottage with a company-starved woman with certain anti-social tendencies, searching out and cleaning three cups amid the litter. I found sugar, creamer, and a lemon in Glory's bag with the tea, and prepped to satisfy every taste.

While I was about this, Glory began the pitch. "If you could trade that ability for something you might find more substantial in life, would you do it?" she asked.

Mother Shipton sighed, reaching for the cup I passed her. "Many's the time I wished I'd not had the Sight," she said. "For I often saw griefs none could forfend against." She took a sip of tea. "Yet, 'tis the source of my income, and as you can see I live well—for the times. And it's been educational as well. I've learned of engineering by building flaws, of military strategies by bad example. I can speak and behave well an' I wish, as I've studied court politics and matters of the heart among the mighty. I've seen the affairs of the Church, the state, the individual, and profited therefrom. Not to mention having developed considerable skills of the combat sort along the way. No, 'tis somethin' of a curse but it's also been good to me. I'd not be lettin' go of it too easily."

She took two more biscuits and a big drink of tea.

"So what you're saying," Glory continued, "is that if you sold your talent the price would have to include something to keep you living in the manner to which you've become accustomed."

"I'm thinkin' it would have to be somewhat better than that. I still have my hopes and the ability maybe to realize 'em. Yes, I would want some small fortune." She looked down at herself, raised a patched outer garment, and let it fall. She ran one hand through her hair and shook her head.

I realized then that beneath the grime her hair was probably blond, with no gray in it. She had striking blue eyes and the high cheekbones of a fashion model. It struck me that she was still possibly in her early thirties, and I wondered what her figure was like under all the wrappings. "I think I'd also like to be good-looking and have some nice clothes," she said, "and have a chance to meet some halfway-decent men."

Glory nodded. "Something might be worked out," she said. "Would you be willing to come with us and talk to the boss? He's in charge of things like that. Don't get the wrong impression. It's not a pact with the Devil. It's all a matter of the natural sciences—and money, of course."

Mother Shipton laughed. "I don't believe in pacts with demons, lass," she said. "I've seen too much about how evil really comes to be. Of course I'll talk with the man and see what he can do for me. If I've somethin' he wants, why that's just good sense."

"'Hunter,'" I said then, nibbling a biscuit.

"Yes, one of the great ones."

"Tell me," Glory said almost casually, "do you get any foreign words along with your visions?"

"Why yes, when they involve foreign matters."

Glory nodded toward me. "Is 'hunter' your translation of something else then, from the feeling?"

"Oh, you're sharp, lass," she said, refilling her cup and quickly mastering the use of a teabag. "There was some foreign tag—somethin' like 'custodian' but it meant 'hunter.'"

"And 'Graylon'?"

"That, too. That, too. Goes with t'other."

Glory nodded and sipped her tea. Her fangs were extruded.

"Mind telling me what the hell you're talking about?" I asked.

"Alf, you're doubtless the most dangerous man on Earth—for centuries in either direction, at that—and you don't even know it."

"Well, how about enlightening me on the matter?"

"No, timing is almost everything in matters of this sort. And there's your timing and there's our timing. And neither has run its course. So we wait and you stew. Just remember that we could have done you harm before now, but we didn't."

I nodded.

"I guess that's the best deal I get."

"The only deal," she said.

"My, this sounds intriguin'," said Mother Shipton; and, fair being fair, I got an idea just then. "And it's just occurred to me," she went on, "that if we spilled a few drops of that brandy into the tea it might be ever so much more excitin'."

Mentally, I tried to recall myself in the mirror for advice. My image appeared in my mind, staring back at me. "Drop your teacup," it said.

I did. Mother Shipton shrieked and her eyes grew moist. Glory said, "Alf, how could you? Little things like that are so dear back here."

"I'm sorry. It just slipped."

Glory stood. "I'll be right back," she said, "with a replacement."

"'Tis not necess—"

Glory was gone. Less than half a minute later she reappeared with a party streamer in her hair and a mug from the Black Place's kitchen in her hand. She passed it to me and I poured myself a refill. "You can drop it all you want," she said. "It's virtually indestructible."

I nodded and we both thanked her. While she was away I'd had time to give Mother Shipton an instruction.

We drank our tea and ate our biscuits. The rain rained and leaked in. Wet thoughts in a gone world.

SIX · MACAVITY'S SMILE

W hen we wished in we were whisked out, which disconcerted me sufficiently that I applied fingertip pressure to La Shipton's wrist as a signal to put my instruction on hold.

In a moment, the scene was recognizable, though it was hardly the parlor of the Luogo Nero. At a table beneath a tree in front of a house the Hatter and the March Hare were having tea, a dormant Dormouse between them, a little blond-haired girl at table's end to their right, Adam across from the Hatter and chatting.

On seeing the direction of his companions' gazes, Adam rose, turning, smiling, nodding toward us. Behind him, the Hatter also got to his feet—tall, familiar—and when he doffed his old-fashioned hat to the ladies his shock of white hair completed the picture.

"My associate, Medusa, whom you just met in passing," Adam said, "is accompanied by Miz Ursula Shipton, a prospective client, and my other associate, Alfred Noir. Friends, permit me to introduce Sir Professor Doctor Bertrand Russell."

"Let us dispense with Teutonic preambling," the man said, showing us a smile. "Happy to meet you, all of you. Adam has not only dealt with the problem I brought him, but has shown me a good time in answer to a secret wish, and handed me a thorny dilemma involving ideals and practicalities." He turned toward Adam once more. "I say, no matter how you try to keep it out it may still find its way in," he said.

"But that argues against your pacifistic principles," Adam responded, "to say that it must develop such a capacity merely from a series of contacts with things human."

"As the days dwindle down and I continue to regard the world about me, probably in worse shape than I found it," the other answered, "I fear that this—this capacity—could be real, though I shall argue against it to my final breath. I am just saying, Don't take the chance."

Adam leaned over and picked up a rod, which I saw to be more than his height in length when he held it upright. It was colored in swirls like a candy cane, and when he thumped it the ground shook, as if he were striking it with a sledgehammer.

"'Be cheerful, sir,'" said he, "'our revels now are ended.'"

The March Hare took out his watch and looked at it. Then he dipped it into his tea and looked at it again. He rose and turned and entered the house, to be followed moments later by Alice and the yawning Dormouse.

"'These our actors, as I foretold you, were all spirits, and are melted into air, into thin air,'" he continued, "'and, like the baseless fabric of this vision, the cloud-capp'd towers, the gorgeous palaces, the solemn temples, the great globe itself, yea, all which it inherit, shall dissolve and, like this insubstantial pageant faded, leave not a rack behind.'"

The house, the tree, the table and all its ware, yea, the sky itself, had faded as he spoke, leaving us in Adam's parlor. Lord Russell nodded. "'We are such stuff as dreams are made on,'" he said, "'and our little life is rounded with a sleep.' But will you break your staff, sir? Will you break your staff?"

In response, Adam raised the rod up over his head, hands far out near its ends, and for a moment I thought he was simply holding it there. Then his back began to broaden and I realized that he was exerting enormous pressure upon the thing. His jacket split down the middle and moments later his shirt tore, too, revealing cables of alien musculature beneath his bronze hide, as the bar yielded and bent. With a twist he had it into an S-shape. Then with additional pressure it became a figure 8.

"I'm not sure about that answer, Adam," Lord Russell

stated, "but thank you for your help as well as your courtesy." Then he, too, was gone.

Adam moved a few paces and leaned the bent rod against the wall. Rising, he seemed to notice the condition of his garments and he grinned at me. Then he faded, except for the grin, which lingered a while.

"How'd he do that?" I asked Glory.

"You mean the fabric of his vision? Left the door to the multi-purpose room open," she said. "It'll spill out if you do that when the mechanism's activated."

"Curioser and curioser," I said, picking up the gaudy figure 8 and satisfying myself that it was real steel. "And the cat's last trick, as in 'Fade to smile'?"

"He was just playing with a side effect of the place," she explained. "Here, inside, the singularity allows you to teleport from place to place. We almost never use it, though. It's easier to walk across the room and pick up a book than to focus the concentration, the will, and the image of place to teleport twenty feet after it. He has a flair for the dramatic, though."

"I've noticed. Still, how'd he manage the lingering smile part?"

"Practice. He's got great control. He's very good at everything he does."

"I've noticed that, too."

And he was suddenly with us once more, standing on the other side of the sofa. He had on a fresh white shirt with his slacks. "Yet are there other revels to attend," he remarked.

"I hope you took sufficient rest," Glory stated.

"Indeed I did, and my youth is renewed like the eagle," he replied.

"Whatever did Lord Russell want to trade?" I asked.

"Halitosis," he answered. "You see, he has a young girl-friend and she recently told him he has bad breath. He tried every sort of mouthwash he could locate, and when none of them did the trick he grew desperate. Then he remembered something Alfred North Whitehead had once told him about this place, and he decided to give us a try."

"And you took his breath away in return for a mad party?"

"I got him to throw in a philosopher's advice, too."

"About life, of course. Always nice to collect a few more opinions."

"About the Iddroid," he said. "He's not sure that our bowdlerization of the Library of Congress will do much good. He thinks that the capacity we are trying to avoid may be built right into that primitive collective unconscious Gomi brought us—which surprised me. It seems to go against much of his general thinking. Still, I'd asked him to speculate as wildly as he would, and he may have found the nature of the project somewhat overwhelming."

He moved around to the front of the sofa.

"It did seem as if you'd shaken him somewhat," I said as he advanced, and I brushed against Ursula Shipton, giving her her cue.

She uttered a cry, rushed forward, and struck him twice, which took considerable courage after she'd seen what he could do to a steel rod. But she was a game lady.

Then she shrieked again and collapsed, rolling back slightly in my direction. I had followed her and I stooped immediately and raised her in my arms. I bore her to the sofa.

As I did, she whispered, "His is the power of the cat. I've

seen him, like at the Last Judgment. He has all of humanity in a box and he's pushing it into the flames. Maybe he really is the Dev—"

"I arranged a little demonstration," I said loudly, "in return for the one you provided me. Scrying by aggression. Go ahead and tell the gentleman something of your vision."

"Nine lives," she said, "and eight hunters to cut their number. The best is yet to be but closes fast. Soon will be the time when you may not land on your feet."

Adam ran a hand through his hair and smiled.

"Rocky," he said. "Yes, you've got it all right." He moved near, leaned and touched her brow. "Let me know when you're up to it and I'll run you through my mall."

"Mall?" she said, eyes widening as she sat up. "I'm ready already."

He took her hand and they headed for the Hellhole.

". . . And a good time was had by all," I said. "Excuse me, Glory. Nature summons."

I made my way to the john fast, closed the door behind me, and stood there visualizing myself at the small room's other end. I summoned my will and desire. Then suddenly I was there. I could do it, too. I teleported back, then back again. I would have to master this, get it down to a reflex, the way Adam had it. I could see that I would have to visit the john often, to practice.

I considered my reflection in the mirror. "Any further instructions?" I asked.

"Not yet," he replied. "Just hang in there. Timing is everything."

I returned to the parlor to discover Glory in conversation with Ashton Ash, no longer an IT, who now wore Levi's, expensive sneakers, a black Italian sport shirt, and a light leather jacket. Sunglasses hung at his belt in an embossed case. He smiled when he saw me.

"I was just saying that I've given it a trial run and it works fine," he told me. "I was wondering whether you people might help me to meet some nice girls now—perhaps ones who've been clients themselves. Thought we might be a little more sympathetic toward each other. Old school tie sort of thing."

"I'm afraid you're going to have to find a lady on your own," Glory said. "We just haven't the facilities to add that to our services."

"But nice girls are hard—"

Just then Adam emerged from the Hellhole with Ursula Shipton, who had disposed of her rags and now wore a black jump-suit and red sandals. Her hair—washed, cut, styled—was indeed blonde, with a red coral clip in it on the left side. She carried a small black sequined purse and a loose-knit red cardigan. Her now-scoured complexion was lovely. I had almost not recognized her save for the cheek-bones and the eyes. She looked even younger than I'd guessed her to be.

"Who?" Ash asked, nodding in her direction.

"A client, like yourself. No, not like yourself," I said.

"Is she married?" he whispered.

"Widowed," I said. "Would you like an introduction?"

"Please."

"Now the money I gave you should last about a week," Adam was saying. "If it doesn't, just come back here when-ever you need more. As a matter of fact, it would probably be a good idea for you to check in here every day, anyhow. That way we can deal with your questions as they arise. I wish I could spare the personnel to escort—"

I cleared my throat.

"Ursula Shipton," I said, "I would like to introduce Mr. Ashton Ash."

He reached forward and took her hand, bowed slightly and raised it to his lips. "I overheard somewhat of your instructions," he said, "and I would be happy to serve as your escort for so long as you choose—starting, perhaps, with lunch."

"Why, thank you," she said, glancing at Adam and at me, "Mr. Ash."

"Just Ash," he said.

"In that case, there are several things you ought to know," I told him. "The lady is from the sixteenth century. This is the distant future to her."

"I understand," he said, "being from a different period myself, even if it is only sixty years down the line."

"Do you know contemporary Rome well enough to show her around?" Adam asked.

"Oh yes. I used your establishment as a Tube stop for some time," he said, "before I got up nerve to consult you on my problem. I'd slink out and explore. And I usually hit this period. I could show her the future version as well as the present one if—"

"I've already seen the future version," she said. "In fact, I've already seen this one. I prefer this one and will probably want to live and conduct my affairs here. I would like to see some of the things close-up, of course."

Adam nodded. Ash conducted her to the door. "I'll give you that close-up view," he said.

"And I'll protect you while you're about it," she told him. "I'll point out the bad neighborhoods as we come to them."

Ash gave me a puzzled look and I smiled and nodded. "She's got a very good left," I explained.

When they were gone Adam laughed. "We *could* open a dating service, you know," he said. "I can think of some very interesting matches from different eras—"

"Forget it," Glory said. "Do favors, but stick to essentials."

"I suppose you're right."

"What did it take to get her looking that way?" I asked.

"Mostly soap and water," he replied, "and a once through the hair, face, and body parlor—for nothing she couldn't have gotten downtown. And a run by the instant garments unit."

"Cheap date," I said. "You're knocking off that list nicely. What kind of body you going to use for the Iddroid?"

"Cagliostro suggested one of the standard android models," he replied. "With everything it will have going for it, though, it should be able to modify itself easily, even beyond the physical."

"It does sound dangerous."

"To be bold is to incur risk."

"What are you going to do with the thing once you've got it?"

"I have major plans, but I'll have to discuss them with Cagliostro."

"I thought you were doing this for him—because it's a snappy project."

"True. But I'd anticipated it. I just didn't have the formula myself. He walked in with it at the right time."

"What if he doesn't like your ideas?"

"He is a reasonable man."

"Let us hope."

"And now, about that long-term memory for you. I say it's time. What do you think?"

"Agree," I said. "You've had me curious for so long that I'm ready to give it a shot. Proust, you say? You've got stuff there from that whole crowd?"

"Oh yes. I gave Charlus—the real Charlus, that is, the Comte de Montesquiou-Ferensac—the temporary orientation for his affair with Sarah Bernhardt, though afterwards he said he'd never do anything like that again. A very demanding woman. Later, Montesquiou wanted some piety. Did you know that he also served Huysmans as the model for Des Esseintes in *A Rebours*? Robert Montesquiou was a man of no particular talent who thus managed a double literary achievement of sorts, and a minor theatrical one. I—"

I was distracted by the appearance of a woman in the foyer at his back. And not just any woman, but one of the loveliest I'd ever seen. She was tall and lithe, with skin the color of dark smoke. She had a mane of natural-looking white hair with black streaks which fell halfway down her back. Her ears were pointed and silver hoops hung in them. Her nails were black and also pointed, her chin small, brow wide. She had on a black cloak over an inches-wide spiral of black material which covered her strategically and seemed to spiral about her at the same time. The cloak's clasp and the anklet above her left foot were of silver. She fixed Glory with her yellow eyes and raised a finger to her lips. Glory nodded slightly. I shivered when she met my gaze and repeated the gesture.

Then she moved, without making a sound, advancing upon Adam's back.

". . . And Robert Haas, the original for Swann," Adam was saying. "He was the nicest guy in the crowd—"

Suddenly the lady vanished. For a moment, I thought she knew the mini-teleportation trick. Then I realized that she had dropped to all fours. She arched her back, and then she lowered it, crouching.

Then she pounced. But even as she did, he was turning, smiling. He caught her in his arms and was borne over backwards by her. Moments later, they were rolling all over the floor making sounds like alley cats.

I moved nearer to Glory and looked at her. "What's going on?" I asked.

"The lady is Prandha Rhadi—'Prandy' for short," she explained. "She's his old girlfriend. They've had this on-and-off thing down the centuries." She crossed to the niche and threw the Switch. "Hate to have a customer come in just now." Adam and Prandy were both on all fours now and seemed at this point to be spitting at each other.

"Are they just being emotional, or would all these sounds happen to be their language?" I asked.

"Both," she replied. "Really, I thought we'd seen the last of her around World War One."

"You don't approve?"

"Of course I approve. It's hard to meet a cat girl around here. It's just that he's always so sad when they break up."

"Maybe they won't break up this time."

"We'll see."

She made a gesture toward the stairway with her eyes. It seemed a good idea and I followed her. At my back there was a rapid exchange of slow, half-growled, half-hissed sounds. Before I reached the top of the stair these were punctuated by several higher-pitched exclamations or statements.

Upstairs, we closed the door to Glory's room behind

us. By then, the sounds of movement had recommenced below.

"What's their story?" I asked, as we both sprawled for a moment on the big bed.

"They met a very long time ago in the distant future," Glory said. "They hit it off very well, too. Then one day they learned that they were each other's designated mates, for purposes of preserving the Kaleideion genes. It seemed one of those cases of really enjoying something until someone tells you you have to do it. Immediately, some spark went out of the romance. Or the whole thing was a powder keg and the spark was ignited. Either way, they quarreled. Now, Adam hadn't told her about this project—the Luogo Nero— and he simply took off shortly thereafter."

"A moment," I said. "Surely they could simply have donated a few cells to the project and continued just as they were."

"Nevertheless, it bothered them. I don't know whether it's simply their mutual neurosis or represents something in the structure of the cat mind itself—not wanting to do what you are told. I know that it wouldn't matter to me or to my species at large, and you Graylons are even said to make a virtue of it—"

I turned and looked into her eyes.

"Oops," she said.

I nodded.

"'Graylon' was one of the words Ursula used about me," I said.

"It means 'human' but there are certain other connotations."

"What are they?"

"You must first understand that a standard model

human being such as yourself is quite rare in the last—that is, distant—future. The ones who have struggled to retain this form are racial purists of the highest sort."

"It would seem as if you cat and snake and mongoose and fox people would have to be pretty much the same way. If you can't interbreed you've got racial purity whether you want it or not."

"True. But with the Graylon—who worked so long at preserving it and enhancing it—there's an ideological component as well. That is, the original human form is considered the best. Others are deemed inferior."

I smiled. ". . . And of course we can't conceive of snakes, cats, mongooses, foxes—whatever—thinking that way about themselves."

She was silent for several moments, then, "Certain individuals of any race are always going to believe that," she said.

"Only when the Graylon do it, it's bad," I said, "because they're probably the devils in your mythology—the dictatorial creators from whom you had to win your freedom. Pride in anything has to be a vice if they've got it."

"They've done everything they can in the way of gene manipulation, cloning, and specialized training to turn themselves into a super-race, one that really is superior to all of the others. The last true humans are self-designed monuments to the notion of superiority."

I laughed.

"How is this so different from you guys winnowing, breeding, selecting, tailoring to produce your Kaleideion? Sounds as if you might even have stolen the notion from those who wanted to see their entire race that way—a fully democratic end within a people. But a Kaleideion? Seems as if they'd like to have everybody goose-stepping—pardon me, pussyfooting—before him. Seems a lot more dangerous than the Graylons' self-improvement program."

"You must all be programmed to think that way!"

"I'm not even willing to admit that I'm one of those guys! I'm just trying to apply a little reason to the claims I'm hearing."

". . . And it's so deeply ingrained that it functions without your even being aware of it."

"I hope you realize you're setting up a no-win scenario for me, no matter what I say."

"What are the highest virtues of a civilized people?" she said suddenly. "Respect for the law? The arts? Devotion to high cultural ends? A dedication to learning the will of the people and promulgating it for the greatest good?"

"I'd be willing to bet it differs from species to species," I said.

"Fair enough. I was drawing generalities from several of them. What do you think the Graylons' ideal might be?"

I shrugged.

"They reasoned that humanity started out as a band of predators, and in one fashion or another remained so throughout history. Therefore, since this was the virtue that made them great, they would enhance it. And they did. No matter what their final individual goals in life, the basic breeding, conditioning, and training of a Graylon is for the hunt. Yours is a race of hunters, Alf."

"So is yours, Glory, or it wouldn't have survived to be perpetuated in your delightful person. All of the species had to be predators in order to survive. That's no big deal. And the cats even throw in a touch of sadism in dealing with their prey. No, you've told me nothing I consider morally objectionable about the Graylon. Is what bothers you the fact that they make open avowals concerning their basic nature?"

"No," she said. "But they send their youths off to hunt the most dangerous beasts in the universe. This is how their career choices are made. And those who show a flair for it become their real hunters."

"The custodians?"

"'Colosodians.' They are the professional hunters, the ones to whom all others turn when there is hunting to be done. They range up and down space-time after whatever they have been hired to pursue. Their prowess is legendary, as is their record of achievement. Pay them enough, and they'll bring back whatever you want, dead or alive."

"The universe has to have its cops," I said.

"A Graylon colosodian is more like a bounty hunter."

"Them, too," I said.

"That's your conditioning talking."

"Or yours. So let's call it even for now. All of this came out of Adam and Prandy's story, which I still haven't heard."

She nodded. "After they quarreled and he departed on this job, she spent a long time trying to figure where he had gone."

"So this is a secret project, outside the quadratic fraternity?"

"Because Adam is the Kaleideion, it was kept very quiet."

"How'd she find him, then?"

She turned onto her side, facing away from me. She reached out and stroked a former self upon the wall. Below, the caterwauling sounds had died away, to be replaced by something softer and steadier.

Finally, she said, "I get the impression she hired a colosodian to track him through time, since they are the best and have their own ways of traveling through it."

I managed to stifle my laugh, turned it into an "Oy!"

"And one day, back in Etruria, she turned up on the doorstep. There was a joyous, tear-filled reconciliation, and they lived happily ever after for a number of years."

"Till they quarreled again?" I asked.

"That's right. She went away then and he was sad for a long while."

"Till she came back."

"Yes."

"And later they quarreled and she left again."

"Yes."

"And this pattern was to be repeated down the centuries."

"Yes."

"It almost sounds like a special mating ritual—taking time off to become a somewhat different person when things grow stale, returning in a new avatar."

From downstairs the new avatars began to wail.

Glory turned back and she was smiling.

"You have a lot of odd insights for one of your kind," she said. "Too bad you're also a bloodthirsty bastard out to kill us for money."

I covered my face with my hands and heaved my shoulders a few times. "I weep," I said. "I weep at all this misunderstanding."

She drew nearer. "You do not," she said. "It's entirely phony. You're not crying."

"No, I'm not very good at it. But at least I'm going through the motions on your behalf—which is totally Confucian and full of respect."

She touched my neck. "Weirdest damned hunter I ever heard of," she said.

"I refuse to be your self-fulfilling prophecy," I stated. "So now what do we have to look forward to from Adam and Prandy? A period of domestic bliss? The lover's inadvertent lobotomizing of a customer when he meant only to remove the quality of perfect pitch?"

"Yes, silly little things like that," she said. "But I've a feeling it won't last. For ages, I've kept track of these things, and this reconciliation is way ahead of schedule. So I made it a point for once to listen carefully to what she was saying."

"'For once'? Are you the mother-in-law figure in the poor girl's existence?"

She hissed long and hard. Then, "Do you want to hear this story or don't you?" she asked.

"Please. Go on."

"She came back," she said, "because of the discovery of a fragment of an ancient historical document which actually mentions this place."

"Got nostalgic, huh?"

"No. But the document indicated that we go out of business about now."

"Say how?"

"No. Maybe on another page. That's the way it is with fragments."

"And of course it didn't indicate what becomes of the proprietor?"

"Right."

I stretched slowly, reached out and drew her to me. "So what's to do?"

"Wait and watch and try to protect him," she said. "I wish I knew more about you." So I kissed her.

Later, looking down upon her, I recalled an old poem I had once written. I recited it:

*"you are different
from any other*

*when I look upon you
I see only you*

*there is no room between us
for flowers
sunsets
moons over water
or the eyes of another*

*the smell and touch and taste of you
have broken that which compares*

*the heat of you has warmed me
and I have heard a song without sound*

*we are different
whatever suns moons
flowers water
or the eyes of others may do*

*the riddle was love
and it has solved us"*

She stared up into my eyes. Then, "I have never heard that rendered into English before," she said.

"What do you mean?"

"It is a famous Eighth Millennium, Pan-Galactic Era love poem," she told me, "applicable to many species. You couldn't have written it."

"I thought I did."

"Even if you were there you couldn't have. Colosodians don't write poetry."

I shook my head and smiled. "Who knows?" I said. "I don't. Kiss me, Glory."

At some point many hours later there came a scratching on our door. I got up and opened it.

Adam stood before me, casually dressed, smiling. "Alf," he said. "I want you to let us out. Would you put on a garment and come down and throw the Switch for us? Prandy and I want to get away, outside, somewhere, for a time, together. Then you can flip the Switch again and sleep for as long as you want."

"Sure thing," I said, snatching up my trousers from the floor, shaking them out, holding them just right, and performing my favorite gymnastic feat. It was seldom I had an audience for it. . . .

Afterwards, our gazes met and held for a moment.

"Most impressive," he said. "That's the first time I've really seen someone put on a pair of pants, both legs at once."

". . . And to answer your question, no," I told him. "The skill is not up for trade. I spent too long learning it when I should have been studying."

I walked him down the stairs, nodded to Prandy, and asked, "Uh, how long you plan on being gone? What I'm getting at is do you want us to be open for business while you're away?"

"Hell, yes," he said. "You've got to throw the Switch sooner or later and get into the timestream just to be able to let us back in. Anyway, you've learned the meet-the-public stuff real well, and Nan will do all the psyche cutting and pasting. She might even start you in on the simpler procedures. It'll be good for you." He glanced at Prandy.

"A few days, perhaps," he added. "Maybe even a week or so."

Prandy nodded and glanced at the door. I reached into the niche and threw the Switch and saw them on their way. Sunny day.

When I crawled back into bed Glory asked me, "What was that all about?"

"They wanted to go off, outside, and be together for a few days."

She yawned.

"Always happens," she told me.

". . . And we're supposed to run the place—maybe further my education in the Hellhole."

"Good idea," she said, drawing me to her. "No problem."

I wondered what she had been dreaming, as there were green stains on her pillow and around her mouth. Venom is like olives, though. You can develop a taste for it.

There was a lot of business in the days that followed. As usual, much of it was mundane and some of it interesting. The ones that light up in my memory are the Case of the Man with the Invisible Appendage, the Woman Who Was Too Acid, the Human-Tuned Portian, the Man Who Broadcast Moods, the Involuntary Teleporter, the Lady Whose Looks Could Kill, the Case of the Double Doppelganger, the Man Who Dreamed Upside Down, the Village in a Rigelian Crystal, the Girl Who Stole Blue, the Seven Bonded Muzwachians and their Unusual Spatial Orientation, the Rudwhorvian Who Was Too Courteous, the Greatest Lover on Peridip, the Vendetta Flowers, and the Bland Augur.

Every day, though, come Rudwhorvians or the absence of blue, I repaired to the john for five minutes or so and practiced my mini-teleports, finally picking up a little facility with them—though I still couldn't manage the smile bit. But smiles could wait for later.

Things went well enough. Glory did let me operate a little, and one day I realized I was actually starting to like the work. Sure enough, though, Glory was upstairs and not available for immediate assistance the day Cagliostro appeared, adding a faint whiff of sulfur and brimstone to the air. He clasped my shoulder and clasped my hand, looking past me the while. "Bonjour, M'sieur. How are you? Is M'sieur Maser in, is *le Maître* in?" he asked.

"Afraid not. Perhaps I can help you, Count."

"Is he expected back soon?"

"I'm not sure when he'll be back. He's taking care of a little personal business."

"*Ah, c'est domage,* but perhaps you will serve," the Count said, turning his attention to me. "How goes our project?"

"Oh, it's coming along very nicely," I told him. "A great number of the ingredients have been collected—and some, as Adam said, were already in stock. I don't think it will be too much longer before he has them all and can assemble the Iddroid."

Cagliostro wrinkled his nose.

"*Son mot,*" he said. "M'sieur Maser's word. I'm not overjoyed with it."

"Why not?"

"It's Freudian. The id is an *ideé* Freudian, the space psychological where the primal sexual energy—the libido—is wild and strong, driving the rest of the mind—"

"I know," I said. "I've read Freud. What's wrong with his term?"

"The psychology of Freud is mainly about the young, people still defining themselves sexually, people whose hormones aren't settled yet. Once their chemistry and their life experiences lay down regular patterns it becomes apparent where the real power lies."

"Jung?" I said. "For the more mature? Individuation and all that? Your collective unconscious *is* a Jungian term. By the way, Adam's found you the one you needed. Traded it off an interstellar headhunter from a million or so years back."

"*Oui?* The man is terribly efficient."

"Yes."

"*Mais non*, it was not Jung that I was thinking of. It was Adler."

"Power drives?"

"Power. *Oui*. The drive to dominate, to command, to be *le premier*, the boss. That's where all the energy *psychique* goes after the youthful sex drives have had their fun."

"Maybe for every psychologist there's an equal and opposite psychologist," I offered.

He chuckled. "*Non, non,*" he said. "M'sieur Alf, look around you. Look inside yourself. Life is all power games. Everyone wants to be the God of something, *tout le monde*. It's just a question of how big a kingdom we can each carve ourselves, how high we can rise."

"So you don't like 'Iddroid.' What do you want to call it?"

"Dominoid," he said.

I nodded. "'Dominoid.' Has a nice sound to it. What's in a name, anyway?"

He slapped me on the back.

"*Vraiment*. Precisely," he said. "Here we are playing word games and we could call the creature 'Fido' for all it matters. The name won't change its nature . . . which, of course, will be Adlerian. May I see what we've got now?"

"I don't know whether Adam would like you looking over his workshop when he's not there," I said. "I think it would be better if you came back in a few days and let him show you the collection himself. I know you'd get better explanations from him, too."

He put an arm around my shoulders and turned me toward the Hellhole. "Alf," he said, "it's not as if I'm some customer in off the street. We're partners."

"True. Still . . ."

"I just want a quick look, one moment."

"All right. Come on."

I took him into the Hellhole and led him toward the work area Adam had set up for this project. Within it, in stasis, hung all of the qualities so far assembled, neatly aligned. The ones that did not lend themselves to visual representation had labeled icons hovering amid their sparkling spaces. To touch any one of them was momentarily to experience it.

"*Merveilleux!*" Cagliostro said. "He's certainly been busy."

"Indeed."

"I wonder whether we might have a little more light? *Un peu?* It's awfully dark in here."

"Adam has found this part of the spectrum and this intensity to be best for him when working with stuff of the mind. But to oblige a partner—" I reached up and unzipped space, drew forth a trouble light, and touched it to life. "What did you want to see?"

"That icon over there. Ah. 'Scrying by aggression.'"

"A recent acquisition of mine," I said.

"I thought you worked for a magazine *americaine*."

"I do. But I decided to cover this properly. I really had to learn the business from the ground up."

"Commendable. *Tres bon!* Where are the controls?" He pointed at the space into which I was stuffing the light. "In one of those pockets?"

A cascade of bleeding wounds flashed upon the wall to my right.

"I don't know what you mean," I said, sealing it off.

"The master controls for the whole business," he said. "This place is a ship, *oui*? I mean the controls by which M'sieur Maître brought it here."

"Oh," I said, recalling Glory's recounting that it had once been some sort of vessel they'd ridden in from the future. "I don't know. It's not relevant for my story."

"They must be around here somewhere, if the singularity's off that way—"

"I wouldn't know," I said. "Why is it important?"

"Oh, it isn't really. *De rien.* I was just curious what they'd look like for something so grand and powerful."

His eyes kept searching and I began to feel uncomfortable. Drifting amputations and strings of organs passed between us, along with a horde of aggressions. "I'm afraid I can't help you. You're going to have to ask Adam about that one, too, when he gets back."

He shrugged. *"Pas important,"* he said. "The body will be placed in stasis here, at the end of the storage field, while we install its attributes, yes?"

"Not really," I told him. "There's a different field for doing such work." I gestured. "It's farther to the rear. We'll set him up there and transport this stuff back."

"Then why is it all up here?"

"Adam is a perfectionist. He set up this special area, away from other business, for purposes of reviewing each quality. He'll move it all back when the time comes."

"Admirable. May I see that other area?"

A love-hate scherzo played suddenly through my breast and a collection of welts on every color skin imaginable flowed underfoot.

I felt myself possessed by a determination that Cagliostro not see the clones. So, "Sorry," I told him. "That's off-limits just now. There's another project underway at the moment back there."

"*Certainement*, I wouldn't disturb it."

"I didn't think you would. By the way, what sort of body is to host this milieu? I think Adam said something about a fancy android from your period?"

"Ah! *Oui*, a top-of-the-line twenty-fifth-century android body known as an adaptoid. It's used for work on other planets and in deep space. It has enormous capacity to change itself: It reads the environment, writes its own specs, and effectuates them."

"I can see why you'd want to remove the Frankenstein factor then," I said. "It sounds as if it could be a tough sparring partner."

"True," he said, "but careful design conquers all."

"Despite Adler?"

He chuckled. "Everybody plays Adler's games. It doesn't make everybody dangerous."

"And if aggressive capacity comes with the turf? If it's hardwired into humans and will accompany any human trait we instill, like a part of the hologram of the rest?"

"My, we are pessimistic," he said, as flames leaped behind him. "Where'd you reach to find that one?"

"Got it from Bertrand Russell."

"Bah! It goes against all his thinking."

"He wasn't proposing it as a thesis. He was examining it as a speculation and offering it as a caution."

"Bertrand Russell! *Mon Dieu!* Who'd have thought he'd get involved in my *petit* project? Still, even if he is correct it does not follow that aggressive behavior will manifest just because the capacity is present. Do you go around striking people you dislike? Of course not. Or not usually. *Non,* there's a difference between the capacity for aggression and the tendency to turn on one's creator."

"—Or father-figure," I suggested. "Terribly Freudian, I admit. Is that why you don't like the idea?"

A mushroom-shaped cloud bloomed on the wall behind him. "That has nothing to do with it!" he cried. "The Dominoid requires a capacity for aggression! We need only prevent its developing undesirable complexes! Such as the Oedipus! We need only keep control of that primal drive! We know how! Enough said." Then he caught himself. "Pardon, I didn't mean the aggression. I meant the power drive," he said.

"Sure," I told him. "But one thing more. Off the subject."

"*Oui?*"

"What's it for? You must have some use in mind for the thing."

He looked away. The cloud at his back collapsed and blew on, to be succeeded by the image of fish nibbling at a floating corpse.

"Mainly research," he said, "into synthetic life. If it meets all our expectations, however, there are some small cosmological observations I'd like to use it for. I'm sure they've occurred to Adam, also, and I don't see how we can be in disagreement—though we must discuss it soon. Thank you for the reminder."

"What sort of observations?"

He glanced back along the tunnel.

"Like the work back there," he said. "Off-limits. After all, you are a writer working on a story, not a true employee. Your tenure here is limited. Let us leave it at that."

I nodded, as the fish swarmed and the corpse vanished. I turned toward the doorway. "Let's head back out then," I said.

"It's amazing, the art displays in this room," he told me.

"A function of the place," I said.

"Have they appeared around me, too?" he asked suddenly.

"You bet. All bunny rabbits and butterflies."

"Oh. I take it they're not really indicative of anything but the general."

"Wouldn't know," I said. "I don't really work here."

After I'd conducted him to the parlor, where he gave Glory, who was there, book in hand, a courtly bow, he squeezed my shoulder and hand again and was gone.

"What was he doing in the Hellhole?" she asked me.

"He wanted to see how far along his project is."

"I wonder whether Adam would have approved?"

"He pretty much asserted his rights as a partner. I could have stopped him if he tried to mess with anything."

"I'm sure you could have. No real choice. No harm done."

"Did Adam tell you what he wants the thing for— above and beyond seeing whether the experiment will work?"

"Yes," she said. Then she smiled.

"Another of those Do Not Discuss things?"

"For now," she said, putting the book aside and stretching. "You ready for more clients? Or you want a break?"

I was in the foyer and had the Switch thrown in a moment.

"Break time," I said. "That was a rough one."

Later, in the washroom, it seemed that my reflection winked at me. Then, "The coin trick, Orrie. Do the coin trick," it ordered, and I remembered.

I dug into my right-hand pocket and removed a handful of coins. Tossing them high, I plucked them one by one from the air and repocketed them, save for the last one—a quarter—which I tore in half.

"Time for you to have your speed back," my voice seemed to say, "so that you can have some time to get used to it again. Hate to dump everything on you at once."

I stared.

"Look," I said finally, "obviously I'm living with a load of masking memories. For how long I've been doing it, I have no idea. They all seem real, and at least some of them must be. Whatever I'm finally to get in the way of real ones, please—don't take away my being a boy in the Bronx, my years at Brown, my friends, my work as a writer. I don't care if they're fake. They're real to me. If there are a lot more I don't know about, yes, give them to me. I'll take them. Give me whatever you want. No complaint. But please, please let me keep these, too, for I just realized how dear they are to me."

Then my eyes brimmed over and my reflection's did the same. No more answers.

I waited for as long as it took, then washed my face and went to look for Glory, careful to keep my speed down.

I found her in her room, stretched out on the bed. She gave me a small smile. "Love is a strange business," she said.

"Agreed," I responded, still standing just inside the door.

"It should make you happy, not sad."

"It should," I said. "In fact it does, me."

"But you won't be with me much longer."

I stroked her nearest skin. "Soon old Alf will be changing his skin, too," I said. "No telling what we might find underneath, eh?"

"Exactly," she said. "You will get all of your old memories and you will become my enemy."

"No. I will not become your enemy."

"Dammy's then. Same thing. We stand together."

"I do not believe you have seen the entire picture."

"But we have evidence and you have nothing."

"I have my feelings, and I do not think I would have them if they were not basically true," I said. "For somewhere inside I know what's going on, and I do not believe that that part of me would mislead this part of me this way."

She laughed. "There are awfully subtle conditioning techniques," she stated, "and the mind is a very malleable thing."

"I know," I agreed, "and I haven't anything left to say on the matter."

"Come here," she said, opening her arms. "I want you while you're still you."

I went to her and sat beside her and looked down at her. Her eyes were big and moist and far apart and wondrous deep.

"You've come here from the end of the universe," she said slowly. "That sword Mother Shipton saw had to be yours. Your destiny is chaotic."

"That may well be the case, but it has nothing to do with your fears."

"The computer was unable to locate an English translation of the poem anywhere," she went on.

"That's its problem, not mine."

"Speak, that I may record it."

I did.

"When I hear you I almost believe you," she said. "But I don't see how it could be."

"Once on a journey I outsmarted myself," I explained, "and I never recovered."

"What do you mean?"

"I'm not sure," I said. "But I remember the constellation you made me—I see it now—and the stars in your eyes are my only destination tonight."

I moved nearer those primal lights and was lost among them.

SEVEN • A MAN OF MANY PARTS

The week that followed was but a continuation of the routine that had gone before, *without* Adam. Certain cases stick in memory: The Whistling Shadow, the Senile Assassin, the Corpse at the End of the Rainbow, the Robot Who Needed a Heart, Those Are Gloves That Were His Hands, and the Unsaintly Stigmatist. Some hard work and

some easy work, punctuated by spells of panic, frenzy, and
madness—between long periods with Glory that made anything worthwhile.

When Adam and Prandy returned, they were arm in
arm and smiling. Prandy was enthusiastic about most places
they had visited, things they had seen. "And Adam is very
famous. One *paparazzo* followed us everywhere, shooting
him," she stated.

"Really," I said. "What did he look like?"

"Oh, short red hair," she replied, "purple and white polo
shirt, sweat pants. Wore mirrorshades most of the time, and
had on studded wrist straps."

"Case of mistaken identity, I'm sure," Adam said.

"No," I said. "No."

"I need a nap," Prandy announced. "Come with me."

"Of course," Adam said.

I met his gaze and held it. "But you've one little promise
to keep before you sleep or get snowed on," I said.

"Oh? What is that?"

Glory entered the room as I replied. "The fancy Proust-
ian memory. I want it now."

We continued to stare into each other's eyes. His shoulders sank and moved forward. "Now?" he repeated. "You're
sure?"

"I'm sure."

Glory was at my side. "Must it be now?" she asked.

"Believe me. It must."

Prandy turned away, releasing Adam's arm.

"It will seem a matter of seconds," she said to Glory.
"Then it will be all over."

"I know," Glory responded.

Adam smiled. "True," he said. "Come along, Alf."

I followed him to the Hellhole and Glory came up beside us. "I will assist you on this one, Dammy," she said.

"No," he replied. "No assistance."

"It'll be all right," I told her.

"I'm going to insist," she said.

He shook his head. "It's not an area where you can insist," he stated. "I'm boss in there. Come on, Alf."

I gave Glory a wink. "See you in a bit," I told her, as Adam opened the door.

She turned away and seated herself on the couch as Prandy mounted the stair. I followed Adam inside and the door closed behind us. We walked through a gentle fall of knives.

"Moment of truth for you," he said.

"I suppose so," I responded, following the fiery claw-marks. After a time, I asked, "Aren't we going back pretty far?"

"All of the really good stuff is stored near the rear," he said. "Aha!"

We had not gone quite as far back as the other Alfs, though I could see them swaying ahead. Adam reached into a small stasis field to his left, and an icon appeared. "Installation will only take a few moments," he said, touching the icon, "though you will be unconscious for a time afterwards. I'm not sure how long, but time means nothing in here."

"When I come around I'll tell you something," I told him.

"Perhaps," he said, and he slapped me lightly on the side of the head and everything went away.

I woke with the taste of madeleine in my mouth. I was standing in a somewhat wider stance than usual, staring back at the doorway. It was still closed, Adam was nowhere in sight, and moments later I realized that something was wrong. The door was upside down. Then I knew that I was standing on the ceiling, though *I* did not feel upside down. In that I felt in no way secured in my position, it occurred to me that I might always have been capable of the feat. I had simply never tried it. I could probably walk right along the ceiling and down the wall. Might as well do it, I decided. I was more used to things below. I raised a foot, began turning to the left.

There was a flash of movement to my right and a sharp pain in that side. Adam had leaped into view, and he had just struck me.

"What gives?" I called, more in surprise than pain.

Another movement, to my left. Another pain, left side this time.

I jumped upward then, drawing up my knees, tucking, spinning through several somersaults as I broke the ceiling's odd grav-field. I could tell that I would not return to it, so when my feet pointed toward the floor I shot them down to it, falling into a low crouch. Partway down I threw a backfist in either direction. My left connected and I heard a soft grunt. I rode the reaction to my right, turning; then I saw a foot coming toward me. I caught it and twisted hard.

I saw the surprised look on Adam's face. I'm sure he hadn't expected me to catch it, but if I did I think he'd anticipated my jamming it and throwing him away. Instead, I pretended it was a steering wheel I was cutting sharply to the left. He extended his right arm then, throwing himself over backward, made contact with the floor with his right hand, and rode the torque I was applying, rotating his entire body along its vertical axis. I switched hands and did it again. This time his left arm went out. . . . I took him in several complete circles in this fashion. I didn't care where he'd picked up these moves—or if he'd been good enough simply to manufacture them on the spot. I knew them by dozens of different names from scores of times and places.

He grinned at me. I straightened my legs, and he stopped grinning as I increased my momentum. Soon he was my unwilling satellite at about shoulder height.

"Why'd you jump me, Adam?" I called.

"You know why—now," he said.

"Nope," I replied. "I've a suspicion, but I'm not sure. Say it."

"Fuck you. I'm the one who toys with his prey."

I let go, continuing to spin several times as I braked.

He tucked and converted his momentum from linear to rotational, presumably ready to meet any surface with hands or feet, rebound, and come at me again. But I'd thrown him amid the hanging clones. When he struck, they fell about him in a heap. I didn't feel like going after him and digging him out. I just stood there and called, "I admit you're tough and beautifully coordinated. Let's call it a draw. We've a lot to talk about."

I heard him spitting. Then he rose from the heap, holding one of the clones—the Vandal, I believe. Suddenly a crew of sexual organs, human and otherwise, appeared, to dance in a ring about him. "Come away, come away, Death," they sang.

Adam tore off the Vandal's right arm and hurled it at me. I caught it and threw it back. By then, he'd twisted off the head, and it was coming my way. Somewhat disconcerting, that, seeing your own features—*caput decapitatum*—flying toward you. Adam ducked the arm and tore at the body again, as the dancing line around him was joined by a staggering line of Lilliputian men and women, zombie-like, each bearing evidence of its death—protruding knives, dangling ropes, rows of bullet holes, the bloated, pale puffiness of drowning victims. They walked the circle in the opposite direction to the dancers and provided a bass line. Adam tore out a handful of intestines and threw them at me as it began to rain blood.

I sidestepped. "Come on! It's not even my clone! What do I care what you do to it?"

He threw what was left of it back over his shoulder, down the passageway toward the singularity, where it vanished. "Why such a dumb lie?" he asked.

"Unfortunately for you, it's the truth. Why such a dumb fight?"

"I wanted to kill you coming into full possession of your memories, so you'd understand exactly why it had to be done."

"Sort of like the guy in Kafka's 'In the Penal Colony'?"

"Exactly. I was sure you'd appreciate it, Alf."

"I don't. You're wrong."

". . . And back in full possession of your fighting prowess—Kaleideion against colosodian. We're both supposed to be the best, you know? Haven't you wondered who really is?"

"Not particularly, Adam. How's about I just yield, you win, and *then* we talk?"

He spat again and bounded toward me. He did have the advantage, though he didn't know it. He could do anything he wanted because he was trying to kill me. I couldn't because I wanted to keep him alive.

Throwing techniques were about as effective on him as

on a basketball. And I knew we could both take a hell of a beating. I wondered who could take the worse one. Then I realized that it didn't matter.

I ducked his first punch and caught him in the armpit with my first one. "A hit! A hit! A very palpable hit!" he announced.

Spinning, he caught me on the side with a hard elbow strike. I tried for the back of his neck, his temple, his nose, his jaw, the side of his neck with five near-invisible strikes while he was low, but he avoided them all. Then he rushed me, arms extended, and I let him catch me about the waist. As I retreated through hanging daisy chains of Lilliputians, I slammed both of my elbows into his temples with sufficient force to kill almost anybody else. Then I did a backward roll and he went away.

I rose quickly and turned, ready to block, evade, parry. But he'd been a little slow in recovering. He grinned as he shook his head, however. "You're better than my coloso-dian practice units," he said.

"I should hope so," I responded, avoiding or sweeping away a few desultory low kicks he threw just to keep the action going. "We made a bundle marketing the things, but it would be too depressing if they were for real."

I made as if to catch at his foot. As he snapped it back I was already moving in, throwing rapid strikes at every possible target. He dodged and parried and blocked, but that was all right. They were only meant to be annoyances. I had decided on a tradeoff.

I landed a rock-shattering blow against his right rib cage. As I did, I felt a similar one against my own. I let him push me away after that, and I caught him on the right thigh with my heel, hard, as I went. "That smarts, Alf. That does smart," Adam remarked, leaning for a moment against the wall and touching his side, shifting his weight to his left leg.

If I had to wear him down with tradeoffs, that was fine with me. I made as if to move in again and watched him wince as he shifted his weight. "I just wanted that sense impression in your files," I said, backing off again.

"I can block it."

"But you won't, any more than I will mine. We've got to keep track of these things to know how the structure's holding up."

"Nailing me would be a big feather in your cap, wouldn't it?"

"Not really. I've nothing to prove."

"I'd always heard you guys were terribly arrogant. It's true."

"Look who's talking: 'Kaleideion against colosodian.'"

Three corpses drifted between us—one dismembered, one with her throat slashed, the other torn almost in half.

"I don't deny it," he said. "There is something glorious about a pair of champions of different persuasions facing each other at the heights of their powers, battling toward that final moment of defeat or triumph."

"If you think this is the fucking *Iliad* you've wandered into the wrong story," I said. "Be a sport. Give me five minutes and I can clear everything up between us."

"I don't want to," he said as he pounced.

He caught me a blow to the side of the head that might have blacked me out for a moment. I remember getting him twice in the abdomen as he did so, though.

Then he had me by the shoulders and slammed me back

into a work area. As my head struck against something very hard, I decided, "Okay. Alf's had enough."

Dizzily, I reached.

I rose from the heap, refreshed, wearing the body of Lars, the Etruscan warrior. Quickly, I moved back toward the entranceway where Adam was banging my Alf body against the tabletop.

Coming up to him quickly, I clipped his jaw with a left, as hard as I could, knocking him back toward the doorway. Then I pushed my Alf-self into the space beside the work area.

"Not fair! Not fair!" Adam cried. "Switching bodies in midstream!"

"To quote you again," I said, "fuck you."

An elephantine dick lumbered by as Adam ran up the wall and onto the ceiling, racing toward me upside down.

He began striking as soon as he was within reach. I didn't have to worry about kicks, though, as he had slowed and lost some measure of control. I stood there ducking and swinging. I felt his nose break beneath my fist. His jaw seemed already broken. A company of bright red cocks passed through us singing "It's a Long Way to Tipperary." I caught him inside both elbows and forced his arms back beyond his shoulders. He bit at me as I did, but I avoided his teeth. With a downward jerk and a full transfer of my weight, I pulled him from the ceiling, which immediately began to drip come upon us. A posse of aggressions raced by, mounted on tired-looking repressions. They pursued the most unusual unicorn I'd ever seen.

Adam landed on his feet, but he was turned partly away from me and he swayed. I nailed him twice on the face again before he adjusted his stance and raised his arms. Then his left hand lashed out with something of his old speed, and his claws took away most of my right cheek.

I kicked him in his right thigh again—same place as earlier—and the leg gave way.

Off to my right, a burning man flickered into existence, looked around, shook his head, and vanished.

I drew several deep breaths. "Somewhere down the line," I said, "I'm going to look up the Kaleideion-makers and tell them what a jerk you've been."

"It took two of you to take me down," he said.

Then, suddenly, his right hand shot forward, resting lightly on the inner surface of my shin bone. His grip was only as strong as it needed to be. The bones at the base of his index finger had fallen unerringly upon the spot about a third of the way up, where a minuscule movement of his hand was about to cause excruciating pain, taking me over backwards, and there wasn't a thing I could do about—

Well, I did a breakfall as I hit, during which time he had also caught hold of my other ankle. He pulled and surged forward. "Most fights do wind up on the ground, don't they?" he said.

Then he drew himself higher and began savaging my big right thigh muscle with his teeth.

I sat up quickly, seized hold of him by the hair, tore his head free of my leg, then bashed it downward against the floor between my legs. As he went still I turned him over and drew him up toward me. I fitted my legs about him from the rear and locked my ankles, holding him in a scissors while I slipped my arms beneath his own and interlocked my fingers on the back of his neck in a full nelson.

"All right. On the ground then," I said. "Wake up quick so I can talk to you. It's important."

Suddenly, there was more light than there had been, and I realized that the door had been opened.

I started to turn in that direction, but she moved quickly. I felt her presence at my back, her hands upon my shoulders. "Release him, Alf, or I'll bite," she said. "Ssso help me, I will." Her mouth touched the left side of my neck.

"Glory," I said, "I have to hold him like this long enough to explain things. Otherwise he'll go wild again. Believe me. Please."

She raised her lips from my neck. "Release him," she repeated.

The light came again, and a voice reached us from the threshold. "Interesting threesome," he said. "Can anyone join in?"

She drew away to look back. I looked, also.

The sharpened studs on his wristbands gleamed, and the colored stripes on his shirt were fluorescent. His hair was the color of blood. Glory rose and stood beside me, facing back. I felt Adam beginning to stir, and I released him. "He is one of the things I wanted to warn Adam about," I said, rising, turning.

He moved forward and I advanced to meet him. At my back, I heard Adam groan.

"It's not nice to jump claims, Orion," the newcomer stated.

I halted before him and raised my right hand, moved it toward him. He raised his right hand and advanced it, also. Protocol gave him the initial pattern. He was my senior, though hardly by much. Immediately, he struck ten death blows at me. I was not allowed to move from my position. I could only block or parry. He was done in an instant, and I threw ten at him. To most normal eyes it would appear as if we had only fluttered our hands by each other in weak salute. This is how colosodii shake hands.

There came a sharp intake of breath from Adam, followed by several coughs.

"I haven't jumped your claim, Eryx," I said.

He gave a brief laugh, then dropped his gaze to my feet and raised it slowly. Then he studied Adam. "Looks as if he actually gave you a good fight," he said. "You would deprive me of everything, wouldn't you?"

He turned and walked on back, then stood looking at Adam. "Can you hear me, Macavity?" he asked.

Adam coughed again, then nodded. "Yes," he said.

"You are under arrest," Eryx said. He drew a sheet of shining white material from his pocket and unfolded it. "This is a copy of the warrant. Care to see it?"

Adam extended his hand. His gaze moved to one place on the sheet. Then he smiled and said, "It hasn't even been written yet."

"Come on. Look at paragraph three. The last great crime in the history of the universe and you think they wouldn't throw in a temporal clause?"

"Always worth a try," Adam said, passing it back.

"I can bring you in alive. I can bring you in dead. Your choice. It's nothing to me."

Adam studied him, then looked at me.

"This is the box and you're Schrödinger's cat," I said. "You're dead, you're alive, you've been arrested, and you've escaped. Nobody outside will know till it's opened again. Whatever happens, though, you go out of business today. We do know that."

Adam drew himself slowly to his feet and leaned heavily on the bench. Eryx faced me again. "As you must know, his is the biggest bounty ever offered in the history of the known universe," he said. "I don't really want to share it. I'd like to know your intentions."

"I'd no intention of getting involved in this thing," I told him. "I was hired by a lady named Pranda Rhadi to locate her boyfriend, who'd skipped town."

Glory hissed and Adam took a deep breath.

"I followed the time-trail to Etruscan Italy," I went on, "and I'd no idea till I ran the ID after I'd found him that it was the same guy who'd stolen the last singularity from the people in the box. When I learned that, I'll admit I was tempted. Who wouldn't be? But I didn't know of your involvement then, and I was curious as to why he'd done it. So I ran the time-line on the Buoco Nero, and I learned that it closes today. He stuck with it for damn near three millennia. How come? What was he up to? I wanted to find out. So I decided to create a full identity here—hypnotic memory suppression and the generation of a totally new personality—that would permit me to fit in with the times and be in a position to observe just what happened in the final days."

Eryx nodded. "I was curious, too, but not that curious," he said. "I ran the time-line, also, and decided it would be just as easy to pick him up at the end as at the beginning. So, *did* you discover what's going on—learn why he drove off in the singularity to open a psycho hockshop?"

I shook my head. "Still not sure," I said. "I learned of your involvement while I was running the line, and I took measures to conceal myself from you. I wasn't sure what I wanted my part in things to be."

"Why didn't Prandy recognize you?" Glory asked.

"Well, I grew a beard and a mustache and I put on some weight," I said. "Mainly, though, I figured that my new personality would provide me with a whole new horde of mannerisms and that they would make the real difference. But I'm not sure that it mattered. She only had eyes for Adam when she turned up here."

Eryx chuckled. "You put in a lot of work on this one," he said. "Now you tell me you're not after the action?"

"I was more interested in understanding Adam's motives."

"If you don't know now, I don't think you'll ever know," he told me. "He's not about to give us anything, and it doesn't really matter. I don't see any special action, and I'm closing the hunt. Schrödinger's box is about to be opened. Now, are you after a piece of the reward or aren't you?"

"What would you give me?"

"Standard finder's fee, just because you kept an eye on him all this time, plus a bonus for softening him up for me—though I didn't ask you to do it."

"No thanks," I said. "I just want to see how it all turns out."

"It's over," he said. "There's nothing to see."

I brushed myself off and stretched.

"I'm not so sure of that," I said.

"What's left?" he asked.

"Ezra Pound's thirtieth Canto."

"What?"

"It's a poem that affected me profoundly when I was in college. I spent days meditating on it. Even went back and read Schiller on naive and sentimental poetry. At that time, I didn't know why it was reaching me that way. Now, of course, I do. You take Adam back, and even if he is the Kaleideion they're going to kill him, or its equivalent."

He nodded.

"So? He knew the chance he was taking when he did what he did."

"I know. But I dislike killing things now. So I decided not to take him in."

"You're a colosodian! We don't have to like or dislike killing. We just have to do it when the time comes."

"Oh, I can do it if I have to, and I still like the hunt as much as ever. I might just become a temporal private eye."

Eryx shook his head. "Do whatever you want. You'll snap out of it one of these days. In the meantime, I'm going to secure the cat-man and take him and this whole damn place back to the end of everything."

Two quick steps and I stood between him and Adam. Eryx halted and stared at me. "You planning on opposing me in this?" he asked.

"Afraid so," I said.

"Then you *are* jumping my claim."

"Damn! I hadn't thought of it that way," I said. "Okay. I am."

"You know I can't let you get away with it."

"No."

He sighed. Then, "All right," he said. "Let's have it out."

A studded wrist strap swept through the air where my head had been but a moment before. I landed a light blow to his throat, avoided three body strikes, and had my left cheek grazed by studs. I was surprised when a double-handed thumb shot to his solar plexus connected and I was able to club the back of his neck, bring my knee up into his face, and deliver a palm strike to the crown of his head. As I did so, I recited:

> *"Compleynt, compleynt I heard upon a day,*
> *Artemis singing, Artemis, Artemis*
> *Agaynst Pity lifted her wail:"*

Rising suddenly, he caught my wrist and threw me across the room. More sophisticated than earlier, I landed upon the wall, ran up it and across the ceiling, and delivered a half-dozen blows to his face before he assimilated the stunt and began fending me off. Moments later, he was attacking, and he caught me on the point of the chin with a blow that knocked me over backwards. Fortunately, it laid me flat upon the ceiling and out of his reach.

He ran up the nearest wall and came racing toward me. But I had recovered by then and regained my footing. I feigned lack of full coordination until he was upon me.

> *"Pity causeth the forests to fail,*
> *Pity slayeth my nymphs,*
> *Pity spareth so many an evil thing.*
> *Pity befouleth April,*
> *Pity is the root and the spring."*

I swept his feet. I kicked him in the stomach twice before he curled into a ball, caught me behind the knees, took me over backwards and rolled over me, trying for my larynx with his forearm. I caught the arm, though, and took him off to my right, following and trying for a choke. I overextended my left arm, however, and he continued turning, locking it straight against him and breaking it at the elbow with a strike he managed by bringing his right foot up, out, around, and in.

> *"Now if no fayre creature followeth me*
> *It is on account of Pity,*
> *It is on account that Pity forbideth them to slaye."*

I attacked his eyes with my right hand and was able to free myself, spring into the air, somersault, and land below. Moments later, he followed, raining blows upon me. I knew that I couldn't hold up much longer.

. . . So I didn't even bother defending against the death grip he was reaching to apply. I simply transferred into the emptied body of Pietro, the artist.

He saw me rise, farther back in the tunnel. "Now that's a low trick, to use a man's own clones against him," he said.

I smiled.

> *"All things are made foul in this season,*
> *This is the reason, none may seek purity*
> *Having for foulnesse pity*
> *And things growne awry;"*

He threw Lars at me and followed with a rush. I retreated, past the place of clones, farther than I'd ever been into the Hellhole. I felt a powerful tugging at my back and determined not to move another inch in that direction. I threw myself flat, and in a moment Lars passed over me like a bullet.

The dark shape gone, I rose again. Eryx approached, arms outstretched, and was almost upon me.

At the last possible instant I teleported eighteen inches

to my left, turning as I did, so that I was able to deliver a stunning blow to the back of his neck as he went by. Glancing back, I saw nothing.

> *"No more do my shaftes fly*
> *To slay. Nothing is now clean slayne*
> *But rotteth away."*

I walked past the heaped bodies toward the front. As I approached, Glory asked, "*His* clones? How could they be his clones? You're the only one they—"

"His face had been damaged and rebuilt," I said. "But he and I were brothers. Twins."

EIGHT · SINGULAR ENCOUNTER

I made my way forward then until I stood directly in front of Adam.

"That, Magfaser," I said, "is why I wanted to talk. It would have saved us both a lot of pain and wasted time. Now I see why you need a nursemaid. You still act like a kid."

"Sorry," he said, "but the circumstantial evidence was strong."

I slapped him across the face, hard, and heard Glory gasp.

He made no move to defend himself. He just nodded and said "Sorry" again.

I turned to my Alf body, saw that it was still breathing.

"Today seems to be the day when everything happens," I said. "Tomorrow you'll be out of business. I wanted my memory today so I could help to make things turn out right."

"I appreciate that," he said.

"Then let's not waste any more time. Summon a medical unit and get yourself put back together. Then there will be a lot of things I'll need to know."

"All right," he said, pushing himself erect and moving toward a work station.

Glory came up beside me and took hold of my hand.

"Sssss," she said.

"Sss-ss," I replied.

"Dammy does not look well."

"I used up several bodies myself," I said. "Listen, Adam kidnapped what was left of the human race, not to mention all the other races who'd decided to try Haven. Why'd he steal the box, Glory? Another misunderstanding?"

"No," she said. "It was their source of power he wanted—that singularity which we knew would be the last one to blow before the Big Crunch occurs."

"I don't understand."

"The effects have all been calculated for ages. He has been filling the cornucopia. And if he takes everything forward and leaves things just as he found them, a second after he removed them, the equations will remain undisturbed."

"But the boxful of downloaded people, the Haveners—all of them banking on living a subjective infinity of time-spurts, there on the brink of chaos—why did he take them, too?"

"To maintain their calculated dose of Hawking radiation and keep the equations pure. They're down in the Hellhole, standing in the same relationship to the singularity as they were when he collected them. It's a simple two-body problem."

"So he really means to return them?"

"Of course! He only borrowed them. He is too neat to interfere with the orderly destruction of the universe."

"He 'borrowed' them for the better part of three millennia?"

"Or for one second, depending on how you look at these things."

"I'm missing something. I'm still missing something," I said. "Like, *why* did he want to borrow the Haveners' singularity, open this place, and run it through the development of Western civilization up until now?"

"Oh, he deals with Easterners, too. You must remember—"

"All right! Conceded! Why? Why?"

"He has accumulated models of all forms of behavior, as well as considerable other information."

"So?"

"He wants the singularity ridden through explosion to Strominger's remnanthood. If a black hole explodes, any information it has taken in is lost to its universe, but Strominger says that the information is preserved in the black hole's horn-shaped remnant in compressed form. Adam plans to return the singularity to the point where he found it, send it forward toward the Crunch till the heavy

Hawking radiation from the last black hole produces the explosion, then see it depart the universe before the collapse."

"It could never return."

"Not to this universe, but it could be directed to its successor. Theory permits its information to be available in that universe—which would become parallel to this—and the information would provide for the development of the anthropic principle."

"Granting he could smuggle information past the Crunch and the Bang, *he* couldn't do it, Glory. Anything material would be destroyed."

"Of course. That is why he was waiting for someone to come along with the design for an infinitely adaptable creature that is both more and less than matter, why he threw himself so wholeheartedly into the collection of the 666 ingredients."

"The Dominoid!"

"Yes, he wants it for the demiurge of our next neighbor universe, driving his cornucopion full of goodies into its earliest history."

"Preposterous. Nothing comes out of a singularity in any condition to discuss information theory."

"He finesses the Crunch and the Bang singularities. Never enters them, never departs. The real trick is for it all to achieve the Strominger Effect and preserve the information. Ultimately, the Dominoid will have to absorb everything here into itself. It is actually to become the cornucopion. And there is evidence it has been done before. In fact, the act may pretty much be necessary for a universe where the anthropic principle obtains."

The entire while we were talking, the healing unit hummed as Adam's manipulated jawbone remineralized.

Another extensor from the unit had reshaped its terminus to flow across his ribs.

"Well, the Buoco Nero closes today," I said. "You know what that means."

"Yes," she replied.

We both turned toward the doorway and moments later it opened. Prandy entered, surveyed the scene, and announced, "Count Cagliostro is here to make a delivery. He asks permission to enter the Hellhole with it."

I looked immediately to Adam, but he was in no condition to speak, to nod, or to shake his head. He gestured for us to approach, and when we did he growled, "Send him in."

"Adam," I said, "if you had the android body could you do the assembly without Cagliostro's help?"

He seemed to reflect, began several answers which proved too complicated, made a twisted face, then repeated, "Send him in."

Glory nodded, turned toward Prandy, and repeated the words.

Prandy held the door wide, and Cagliostro—in his big, red, Mephistophelean mode—entered the Hellhole, grinning nastily, a body bag slung over his shoulder. "Well, well, well," he observed, "this looks like the last chapter of a *histoire étrange* here—or the first."

Advancing, he deposited the bag at Adam's feet. "Here's the host, M'sieur. Are you ready to proceed?" he asked.

"Will be. Soon," Adam managed.

Prandy moved to Adam's side, took his hand. "What happened?" she inquired.

"Later," Adam said.

I moved forward and stood beside Cagliostro. "Unpack

it, and I can help get things ready while we're waiting," I said.

"Good idea," he replied, leaning forward and unfastening the bag, working it downward on the android. It was possessed only of feature buds, was hairless, sexless, and very cool to touch, its skin translucent to the point where it seemed almost to glow. Faint outlines of internal structures were visible within it.

"Let's move it down to the adding field and I'll set it up," I said. "I could also bring up some of the ingredients, but I've a feeling there's a special order to their installation."

"That's right."

We both took hold of the body and I led the way. It was surprisingly light. I laid it down in the field in an easy-access position. A small stream of blood seemed to be flowing down the center of the tunnel toward the rear.

Adam removed himself from the healing unit and came over. There was a certain puffiness to his face, indicating that he should have waited longer. "Let's be quick about it," he said.

"*Oui*," Cagliostro replied, rubbing his hands together. When he drew them apart they held a parchment scroll between them which he unwound for several inches. "We begin with the peripherals," he stated.

"All right," Adam said. "I'll assist. Read ahead on the list and the others can fetch ingredients and have them ready for us as we need them."

Deep-voiced, Cagliostro began to read—or rather intone—the first part of his catalog. Glory, Prandy, and I began to scavenge, bringing back the factors that would produce the Beast. Some were ready and easy to locate; others, Adam had not had opportunity to assemble in one place.

Nothing occurred at first as Adam and Cagliostro went about their business using the adding field to install qualities in the Dominoid. Several dozen were actually added to its makeup before its color grew brighter and its fingers twitched. As the process advanced, the feature buds took on firmer resolution. Suddenly there were eyes, albeit closed. The small, central facial bump had grown into a large, somewhat flattish nose. The mouth was no longer a thin crease below it.

We continued. After a time the chest heaved and the hands clenched and unclenched. Cagliostro's voice called for more ingredients and we scrambled to furnish them.

"I'm not sure I like this thing," Prandy said.

Flames climbed the nearer wall and faded, to be succeeded by wheeling galaxies. The Dominoid seemed to have gained additional length and brightness. Its eyelids fluttered for a moment but did not open.

Tiny bat-winged creatures swooped by. I heard the call of an owl. A gentle rain, like molten gold, began to fall across the starry prospect. Glory passed more ingredients to Adam. I gave the next batch to Cagliostro. Cagliostro unrolled the scroll further and read off more items. Prandy brought him several. The Dominoid made a small, whimpering sound. A beat like a roll of thunder passed down the Hellhole.

Time was without meaning as we fetched and delivered. I had no idea how many of his needed qualities the Dominoid had acquired. "Now, the Library of Congress," Cagliostro ordered, and this was done. The Dominoid groaned, and Cagliostro halted the procedure to inspect it. Satisfied, he read off another series of items.

The eyes opened for a moment—a blazing blue—and were squeezed shut immediately to the accompaniment of an inhuman shriek. Liquid and bright, like metal in a crucible, its skin seemed almost to be flowing.

It groaned again and tried to sit up. Adam and Cagliostro continued their work. Steam began to rise from the surface of its body. After a while tiny charges of static electricity danced across its torso, among its toes.

"How far along are we?" I finally asked.

"Almost finished," Cagliostro said. "Soon. Soon."

The Dominoid succeeded in sitting up, tried to rise to its feet. Cagliostro pushed it back down. Its eyes opened suddenly, staring into his own. "*Oui, mon cher,*" he purred. "Soon."

The Dominoid's lips moved. "Mother?" it said.

Cagliostro laughed. "Why not? I am your mama"—he gestured at Adam—"and this one your midwife. These others assist us."

The Dominoid reached out with its right hand and stroked Cagliostro's cheek. "Mother," he repeated. Then his gaze turned to Adam and he took hold of his hand and squeezed it. "Midwife," he said.

Adam smiled. "I am honored," he stated.

Cagliostro reached forward and installed the 666th ingredient.

"*Maintenant* you are perfect, *mon petit,*" he said, reaching out and placing his fingertips upon its temples. "Can you see where the main controls to this place are situated?"

"Of course. Forward and to the right." It gestured. "I will take you to them."

"No. Just do as I do. Place your hands upon my head as mine are upon yours."

The Dominoid's hands moved forward, fingers touching Cagliostro's temples. They stared into each other's eyes.

"No!" Adam cried. "Stop them, Alf! I never thought—"

I was already moving.

Still smiling, Cagliostro moved his right hand in a fairly sophisticated gesture which would have brushed many people aside. He was surprised, therefore, to find all of his fingers broken; and he lost his smile as I applied a wristlock which took him over backwards.

"Alf! Lay off! Prandy! Hit the ground!" Adam called then.

I drew back and Prandy dropped. Cagliostro continued to roll backwards and came again to his feet. He regained his smile as he did so. "Really—" he began.

There was a blur in the air and a high-pitched hum as something dark and well-antennaed settled upon his shoulders. There was no scream, though, over the buzzing that ensued. And as Cagliostro's headless corpse fell to the floor, I heard Gomi's voice say, "I feel ahead on this deal. Yo ho ho!" Then, with the sound of a closing canister, his grotesque shadow flashed away and was gone.

"Sometimes your timing is quite good," I said to Adam.

"Can't lose them all," he replied.

Then the Dominoid stood up, still glowing and steaming, still flickering and flashing in places. Its lips had moved into a small smile. "Too late, *mes amis*. Too late," it said, and it began to move toward the rear of the Hellhole.

"Well, maybe you can," Adam amended, leaping into its path.

There was a brief encounter, masked from me by the creature's back, and Adam was cast off to the left, slamming against the wall. "I anticipate you," the creature remarked. "Could it be otherwise?" It continued on its way toward the rear.

"Alf!" Adam yelled. "Get it into the stripping field if you can!"

I bounded forward, leaped so as to strike the right-hand wall feet-first, continued on to the ceiling to arrive upside down above the Dominoid, one hand taking hold of it beneath the chin, the other upon the top of its head. I tried snapping its neck to its right. With a standard model human the neck anatomy is such that successful resistance in that plane would make it vulnerable for a front-to-rear break—and vice-versa. But it did not resist. It received my maneuver with a range of movement exceeding the human. A greater plasticity allowed for it to follow the full extent of my attack without suffering any damage.

Its hands moved upward and took hold of my wrists. As I was facing the front of the Hellhole, I immediately pushed off and dropped down, arriving on my feet behind it, my turning movement raising its hands to shoulder height. I freed my left wrist with a twisting movement, placed it atop its right hand, which still had hold of my right wrist, and tried to bring it back over its shoulder and down for a take-down. But it turned slightly toward me with a backward movement of its right foot, lowered itself slightly, and stepped forward again, spinning me past its right side to face it. Its wrist should have given way as I was propelled about it, but again that plasticity preserved it, as I felt it loosen and stretch within my grip.

My right foot was against its abdomen as soon as it was within range, and I kept turning, keeping the tension on its arm, pushing with my foot, and dropping to the floor to my left. Its balance broke and it shot forward above me.

We recovered our footing simultaneously, and I heard Cagliostro's laugh emerge from the lips of the Dominoid. "Alf! You are a colosodian! *C'est magnifique!*" he said. "No one else could have done that! You have granted me a long-time wish to see one of you in action!"

I was already attacking by then, this time with techniques designed to dismantle robots. "But this must not continue," he said, and his shimmering, creamy color, touched with gold, was muted.

My first blow passed completely through him, as if he were made of smoke. So did a rapid sequence with which I followed it. He turned away then, saying, "I must be about my business."

"And what might that be?" I inquired, following him along the claw marks past the heaped clones.

He halted in advance of them, faced the right-hand wall, extended both hands, and, like a parting of curtains, opened a section of space. An elaborate control panel hung before him. "Ask Adam," he said.

I turned toward Adam, who had also opened a compartment in seeming nothingness and withdrawn a thirty-inch tube with a bore like a bazooka. He held it at his right side and gestured with his head for me to move out of the way.

I did, and Adam triggered the thing.

The Dominoid, just leaning toward the controls, halted and stiffened. Its outline wavered, blurred, as it began to vibrate. A humming from the weapon rose to a wailing. The tableau held for several seconds, then its outline grew more stable. Adam immediately touched a control on the weapon's side and the Dominoid blurred again, a great gust of steam rising from it.

. . . And again the shining being stabilized, its form growing clearer. Adam touched the control several times in rapid succession. The pitch of the wailing rose and fell, but that was all that changed. The outline became totally crisp as Cagliostro's voice came again: "Too late. I can vibrate in any fashion it can, and I can respond immediately now. Put it away, Adam, unless you have nothing better to do."

Adam licked his lips, tossed it back into the niche, and sealed it inside as I came up next to him.

"What's the big deal?" I said softly. "He's going to do what you want done anyway now, isn't he?"

Adam nodded slowly, then shook his head. "Yes and no," he replied.

Prandy came up and rubbed his shoulders. Glory was at my side.

"It never occurred to me that Cagliostro might transfer his consciousness to the Dominoid," he said. "It was still in a sufficiently disorganized state that he was able to move in and dominate it completely."

I felt a moment's queasiness as an odd vibration jarred me. Looking back, I saw that the control panel was glowing with several colors.

"Still," I said, "he's providing direction. What's wrong with that?"

"The demiurge becomes, in effect, God," he said, "in the next universe. He can impose his will in many ways upon initial and subsequent conditions."

"Oh," I said, and it seemed we were turned inside out and spun, along with everything about us.

Cagliostro's voice rang in my head. "The last journey begins," he stated.

I awoke to a pumping feeling, within and all about me. When I opened my eyes, I saw that Adam, Prandy, Glory, and I were sprawled on the floor, walls, and ceiling, respectively. The Hellhole and our own bodies seemed to phase into and out of existence with each pulsing of the place. I heard Glory hiss, and Prandy groaned. A moment later, there came the annoying high whine of a UHF communication. I looked down at Adam and saw that he was sitting up. I did the same. Then I sprang, landing beside him.

"To continue," I said, "why don't we have a detectable God in our universe? You said they're almost indispensable."

"Oh, they wear out after a time," he replied. "Actually, you met ours. You gave him a bottle of wine."

"Old Urtch?"

"Yep. He was once the Big Guy."

I shuddered. I watched Glory uncoil into a standing position on the wall. I noticed that the pulses seemed to be coming further apart.

"We're slowing," Adam said, moving to the opposite wall where he helped Prandy to her feet. "We're approaching the moment at which I acquired the singularity and the Haven."

"What happens then?"

"He will position us, then accelerate to the final singularity. We will brush by the Big Crunch and depart the universe."

"And?"

"We will die, but the demiurge will change its state and continue on. At least another anthropically-endowed universe will come of this, no matter how warped. That is something to be grateful for. Perhaps analogues of ourselves will exist within it, in some form."

"Is there nothing left to do?" I asked.

"There is always something to do," he said, reaching down and unzipping another area of space. "In this case, we celebrate. I've several cases of champagne in here."

There came another slow pulse as he opened it fully and a cascade of empty bottles rolled out followed by the tatterdemalion figure of Urtch, a bottle still clutched in his hand.

"Eh! Eh! What's going on?" Urtch inquired.

"We're approaching Omega minus one," Adam answered.

"You might have told me," the ancient demiurge responded.

"I didn't know you were in there drinking my champagne."

Urtch smacked his lips and smiled. "And very good champagne it was," he said. "A nineteenth-century Veuve Cliquot, I believe." He rose to his feet and brushed himself off.

"You didn't even leave us one?"

"I don't know. Didn't realize it was in demand." He gestured back toward the controls. "That the new demiurge?"

"Sort of," Adam replied.

"What do you mean 'sort of'? Either he is or he ain't."

"Well, he was. But then another entity took him over within moments of his birth. *He* wanted to be the demiurge."

"That ain't right," Urtch said, wiping his mouth on the back of his hand and belching lightly. "That ain't how it's done."

"I know. But there's not much I can do about it."

Urtch rolled his eyes, in two different directions.

"Damn!" he said then. "Thought I was done with all this foolishness." He straightened his garments. "Guess I'll have to set things right."

"I don't think you're a match for him," Adam said.

"Experience counts for something," Urtch told him, and he turned and shuffled off toward the control section.

As he faded into and out of existence he began to glow faintly against the shadowy background. The pulses slowed even more, achieving full stoppage just as he touched the Dominoid's shoulder and said, "Excuse me, sonny."

"What—?" Cagliostro asked, turning toward him.

Urtch moved forward and embraced him. "Family," he said. "Family."

They stood so for several moments, and both of them began to steam to the point of indistinctness.

Then, "No!" Cagliostro cried. "You can't—"

"Yes, I can," Urtch said.

When the steam had fled only a single figure stood before the controls. It was that of the Dominoid. It turned then and waved at us. "Never thought I'd have to run the show twice," Urtch's voice came to us. I rushed to my Alf body even as he continued, "You folks got any way of getting back home?"

Removing the cuff link case from my pocket, I opened it and tore out the lining to reveal the control board for my tiny time-machine. "This is the best I have with me," I called out.

"Let's see it."

I carried it back to him.

He took it from me and studied it. "Dinky little thing would take you a billion jumps to get back there," he stated.

"I know. It was just for getting me to and from my ship, within the century," I said.

"I'll have to hype it up for you so you can do it in fewer steps than that," he said, clasping it with both hands and making it glow. He handed it back to me. "Okay. Better get on with you. I got it all to do over again."

"Uh, thanks," I told him.

I turned and rushed back. Adam was on his hands and knees, rummaging in the space pocket from which Urtch had emerged. "He missed two!" I heard him say. "We can still celebrate."

I raised Alf and slung him over my shoulders in a fireman's carry just as Adam popped a cork. We all moved close together. Urtch made a strange gesture to us and returned his attention to the controls. I activated my own.

We jumped backward from Omega minus one.

"Cats on the rooftops, cats on tiles!" Adam sang as we landed on the windswept plains of a dark world near a faintly-glowing, deserted city. He passed a bottle and then we jumped again. It's a long way to Tipperary.

. . . A dim, dead sea bottom near the dried-out hulk of an ancient vessel.

Alf the sacred river ran.

Backward

turn

backward

O

Time

in

your

flight

bring

back

my

Roma

for

one
shining
night

We held each other up and sang of strings and sealing wax as the stars were switched on again.

It's the wrong way to tickle Mary. . . .

"'Hssssssssssssssss-sssssssss! Ssssssssssssss! Sssss-sss!' 'Tis the song the first snake sang, there in her tree," she said.

"You know there are two real endings—one where we had to stay and accompany him as data, like the Haveners."

"'Seventeen bottles of beer on the wall . . .'"

And the light of our day, flashpoint to it all:

NINE · NUOVO BUOCO NERO

It took us the better part of the year—there, twenty years forward from our time of departure—to wrestle the Martian singularity a sufficient distance away for our purposes, using my invisible stalking cruiser, and to connect it by warp to the shell of the old Black Place. And it took months to install the amenities, such as the Switch. I made a quick run far forward for some parts for the setting up of a new multi-purpose room. I'd grown attached to the idea of having one around. We all worked to set up the office.

Alfred Noir, Glory M. Duse,
P. Rhadi & Adam Maser
Confidential Investigations
Anywhere, Anytime

it read, on the frosted glass of its front door. Its two side doors say the same thing, but the outside of one is located in San Francisco, the other in New York. I can always move them around if business is slow, but it hasn't slowed yet. So far, we've successfully handled the Case of the Chuckling Man, the Voice of the Armadillo, Six & a Half Dead Long Islanders, King of the Cable Cars, North to Syracuse, and the Phantom of the Napa. I love a mystery.

Adam and Prandy, in their spare time, have just about completed work on a passage strangely similar to the Hell-hole. I have asked them whether they mean to get back into soul-changing and try for a second universal continuance—I'm not sure I'd help to build a better Beast—but Adam just shrugs and mumbles something about old times. Cats are inscrutable. The place is, however, perfect for stor-ing my spare body. Alf or Pietro, it's sometimes nice to be able to switch back and forth when the action gets fast and let the other do my sleeping for me, or recover from a bullet wound, sleep off a hangover, or a cold. In fact, the others have just about decided it's time they had spares, too.

. . . And Glory reads my poetry. I recently wrote a piece wondering whether some recorded portions of ourselves made it through with Urtch and what might have become of them.

Excuse me. There's somebody at the San Francisco door. Casts an odd shadow. But who cares, so long as they've got the retainer and the dailies?

ALSO BY ALFRED BESTER

"Alfred Bester was one of the handful of writers who invented modern science fiction." —Harry Harrison

THE DEMOLISHED MAN
With a New Introduction by Harry Harrison

In this classic science fiction novel, the first to win the prestigious Hugo Award, a psychopathic business magnate devises the ultimate scheme to eliminate the competition and destroy the order of society. Hurtling from the orgies of a future aristocracy to a deep-space game preserve and across densely realized subcultures of psychic doctors, grifters, and police, *The Demolished Man* is a masterpiece of high-tech suspense.

Science Fiction/0-679-76781-9

THE STARS MY DESTINATION
With a New Introduction by Neil Gaiman

In this pulse quickening novel, Alfred Bester imagines a future in which people "jaunte" a thousand miles in a single thought, where the rich barricade themselves in labyrinths and protect themselves with radioactive hit men—and where an inarticulate outcast is the most valuable and dangerous man alive. *The Stars My Destination* is a classic of technological prophecy and timeless narrative enchantment.

Science Fiction/0-679-76780-0

VIRTUAL UNREALITIES
The Short Fiction of Alfred Bester
With an Introduction by Robert Silverberg

Nowhere is Alfred Bester funnier, speedier, or more audacious than in these seventeen short stories—two of them previously unpublished—that have now been brought together in a single volume for the first time. Read about the sweet-natured young man whose phenomenal good luck turns out to be disastrous for the rest of humanity. Meet a warlock who practices on Park Avenue and whose potions comply with the Pure Food and Drug Act. *Virtual Unrealities* is a historic collection from one of science fiction's true pathbreakers.

A Vintage Original
Science Fiction/0-679-76783-5

CENTRAL

DATE DUE

GAYLORD   PRINTED IN U.S.A.